The Outlaw Legend Begins

Butch Cassidy and the Sundance Kid have given up robbing banks and trains and are now ranch owners, and are waiting to hear from the Governor of Wyoming about a possible pardon. While in Buffalo, Wyoming, to buy supplies, they have an unfortunate encounter with Luther Greeley, an outlaw from a rival gang based at Hole-in-the-Wall, during which Sundance is badly wounded. Butch takes him to the nearby home of a friend to recover.

As a worried Butch watches over his injured partner, he thinks back to their first meeting and to the events that led up to their partnership. It all began in the town of Green River, Wyoming, and a chance meeting between them when they were young, then using their names Leroy and Lonzo. . . .

The Outlaw Legend Begins

Saran Essex

A Black Horse Western

ROBERT HALE

© Saran Essex 2018
First published in Great Britain 2018

ISBN 978-0-7198-2698-6

The Crowood Press
The Stable Block
Crowood Lane
Ramsbury
Marlborough
Wiltshire SN8 2HR

www.bhwesterns.com

Robert Hale is an imprint
of The Crowood Press

Typeset by
Derek Doyle & Associates, Shaw Heath
Printed and bound in Great Britain by
CPI Group (UK) Ltd, Croydon, CR0 4YY

For Floss, Sandy, Jason and Roxy

CHAPTER 1

Robert Leroy Parker, alias Butch Cassidy the outlaw, knew that the brown-haired, scar-faced man had recognized him. It was a pleasant afternoon in Buffalo, Wyoming, sunny and dry, and with a light mist over the mountains.

Luther Greeley had been crossing the street as Butch was strolling along the wooden sidewalk towards the livery stable to meet up with his partner, Harry Alonzo Longbaugh, alias the Sundance Kid. Greeley's sullen, deep-set eyes had glowered straight into Butch's own, but then the man had turned away, and walked on down the street without doing or saying anything – but Butch was certain that Greeley had recognized him. A couple of years earlier, Sundance had beaten Greeley to a draw and wounded him in the shoulder, and Greeley had sworn revenge on him.

Luther Greeley was an outlaw and a cruel man. He used to be a member of an outlaw gang that was based at the remote hideout of Hole-in-the-Wall, Wyoming, at the same time as Butch and Sundance and their gang also used the hideout. This outlaw gang was envious of Butch and Sundance's success with their robberies, and of their fame, and had often tried to pick fights with them, especially

Greeley; Greeley was also resentful of Sundance's reputation of being fast with a gun, and had challenged him to the draw.

Butch knew that the venomous and black-hearted Greeley was not the kind of man to forget about the incident, and that he would gladly shoot both Butch and Sundance in the back without any qualms.

Butch and Sundance were in the town of Buffalo to buy supplies. The two men were outlaws and were wanted by the law, but they were also the owners of Bitter Creek Ranch in the Big Horn Mountain country of Wyoming, and for more than a year had not carried out any bank or train robberies. They were waiting to hear from their governor friend, Jacob Hurley, about a possible pardon being granted to them in Wyoming.

Their feelings regarding the pardon were mixed. They enjoyed ranching and were proud of their ranch, which had been left to them by a deceased friend, but the two of them knew that, deep down inside, they both possessed a bold and restless spirit, and that adventure and risk taking was what they loved best. Sooner or later, the need for adventure and danger would become too overwhelming for them to resist – but for the time being, they were law-abiding ranchers. Maybe they would get the pardon and settle down to an honest way of living – but it was a big 'maybe'.

Butch had carried on walking up to the livery stable after his surprise encounter with Greeley, but he didn't find Sundance waiting either inside or outside the stable. The partners had split up after buying the supplies they needed: Sundance had gone off to pay a visit to a lady friend of his who worked at a hotel in the town, while Butch had gone for a wander round the town and to speak to some of his friends. Butch and Sundance had friends in a lot of towns and places in the west and in other areas of the country, and in every kind of business.

Butch stared anxiously up the street. He wasn't a man who panicked, but even so, he would be glad to get out of town, and away from Luther Greeley. He breathed easier when he caught sight of Sundance sauntering along the sidewalk towards him. It may not have been obvious to anyone else, but as Sundance walked nearer to Butch, he could tell just by looking at Butch's stance that something was worrying his partner.

The two men had a unique bond of friendship. They were kindred spirits and could easily read each other's thoughts. They had been through a lot of dangerous situations together, and they now thought of themselves as family, and would willingly sacrifice their lives for each other.

'I just saw Luther Greeley!' Butch said in an urgent tone to The Kid as Sundance reached him, 'Let's get out of here!'

Butch always tried to avoid trouble whenever possible. Like his partner, he had a completely fearless nature, but unlike Sundance, he did his best to avoid confrontations. Sundance wouldn't start a fight, but if someone else wanted one, then he would happily oblige them.

Sundance glanced around the street to see if there was any sign of Greeley. All he saw were a few of the town folk going in and out of the varied stores and saloons on both sides of the dusty street, and horses tied to the hitching rails. He was frowning, however, as he followed Butch into the stable. His uncanny instincts were telling him that Greeley might be hiding somewhere and watching them.

Butch and Sundance led their horses out of the stable. Butch quickly jumped astride his mount and urged Sundance to follow. Sundance groaned to himself; he was in fact quite willing to face up to Luther Greeley, though he understood how Butch felt. He wouldn't intentionally do anything to cause anxiety to his partner, and maybe Butch's thinking was right: the town of Buffalo wasn't a good place for a confrontation of any kind, especially if they wanted to get the pardon.

Sundance swung up into the saddle, but he still couldn't shake off the feeling that Greeley might be watching them from some hidden vantage point. He took a quick look behind him before urging his horse to follow after Butch, who had started to ride away. The street, Sundance noticed as he glanced behind him, was now fairly deserted – just a couple of men walking along the wooden sidewalk – but Sundance purposely kept his horse back behind Butch: he wanted to be able to protect his partner if Greeley did suddenly spring out behind them and start firing.

Having caught Butch's eye with his penetrating stare, Luther Greeley had pretended not to recognize him, and had carried on walking down the street – but unbeknown to Butch, he had dashed down a side alley and waited. He had hidden behind some barrels, and watched as Sundance strolled past the entrance to the alley on his way to the livery stable. He could have opened fire on Sundance at that moment, but he wanted to kill both of

9

the outlaws, and he wanted to wait until they were together before springing out from the alley to surprise them and shoot them down.

A split second after Sundance had glanced behind him and, having seen no danger, had started to ride after Butch, Greeley sprang out of the alley. He stood about ten feet behind the departing outlaws, and with a malicious grin on his face, aimed his gun and fired twice. The bullets whizzed over their heads, and Sundance instantly swung his horse around to fire on Greeley.

Some curious and concerned townspeople, having heard the gunshots, emerged out of doorways on to the street. Among them was the town sheriff. Sundance's keen eyes had quickly spotted the townspeople and the sheriff emerging into the street, and he did not shoot to kill or even to injure Greeley, as the last thing he wanted was an irate sheriff and posse giving chase after him and Butch. He therefore fired two rapid shots at Greeley's feet.

The bullets kicked up dust and dirt. Greeley stepped back a pace and opened fire once more. His gun spat flame almost at the same instant as Sundance also fired his weapon again. Sundance's bullet struck the ground near to Greeley's feet, kicking up more dirt and dust that flew into Greeley's face and eyes, causing the man to cough and rub his eyes. But Greeley's bullet struck Sundance in the chest.

Sundance gasped with the shock and the sudden, intense burning pain. Blood started to gush out of his chest wound. When Butch heard his partner gasp he pulled up his mount and looked back at him in alarm.

'*Sundance!*' he cried out.

10

Sundance ignored the searing pain that was raging through his chest and yelled at Butch to keep riding, but Butch refused to do so: he wasn't going anywhere without his partner. Sundance knew this, and he also knew that to keep Butch from possibly getting shot by Greeley, he would have to try and cover up the fact that he was maybe badly injured and losing a lot of blood.

He kept his arm in front of his chest as he rode up closer to Butch so that his partner would not see the blood, and he tried to avoid Butch's eyes. He nodded to Butch to indicate that he was fine, and the two men spurred their horses into a fast gallop.

Greeley stopped coughing and rubbing his eyes to fire a shot after them. The town sheriff, holding his gun in his hand, came running up the street behind Greeley, and shouted at him to stop shooting and to drop his weapon. Greeley, foolishly, spun round on the lawman, ready to open fire – and the sheriff shot him through the heart.

Butch and Sundance had been riding for nearly five miles since leaving Buffalo, and increasingly Sundance, weak from loss of blood and in considerable pain, was unable to keep up the pace. He was dropping further and further behind Butch, and was so weak that he was almost falling from the saddle. Butch soon became aware that he couldn't hear The Kid's horse galloping hard behind him, and as he turned his own horse around, he saw the distress that his partner was in. Fear was tearing at his heart as he galloped up to Sundance. He reached over and caught hold of his partner before he fell from his horse.

'*Sundance!*' Butch breathed out in alarm when he saw

the blood gushing from the hole in Sundance's chest, and cursed himself for not realizing how badly hurt he was. He should have known that his partner would try to hide his injury so that they could get away from Greeley.

Holding on to Sundance, Butch knew there was no time to lose, that his partner's wound needed urgent attention. Luckily there was a place about a mile to the east of their present location where he could take Sundance to have his wound taken care of, a small homestead belonging to Jerome Arnott and his wife and young son. Arnott was a friend of the two outlaws, and he had worked as a doctor's assistant in the past.

They had to ride at a walking pace, and Butch had to hold Sundance in the saddle the whole time, so for Butch it seemed hours before they reached Arnott's cabin. Outside the cabin door Butch called out for help, and fortunately Arnott heard him and came running out. The now unconscious Sundance was carried into the back bedroom where Arnott's young son, Tommy, slept, and was placed on the boy's bed. Tommy was ordered out of the room while Arnott and his wife, Ellen, examined Sundance's wound.

It was found that the bullet had cracked a rib in The Kid's chest, but had luckily missed vital organs, and had made its exit out through Sundance's back. Arnott bathed the injury with hot water, then stitched it up, and bandaged Sundance's chest.

As Butch watched Jerome tending to his partner, he felt immense waves of fear surging through him. He knew how badly hurt his friend was, and he could not face the possibility of losing him.

'Will he be OK?' Butch asked shakily, when Arnott had finished the bandaging.

Arnott's eyes were grave as he looked at Butch. He had known the outlaws for a few years, and they had been good friends to him and his family. They had worked for Arnott on his homestead, and had asked for nothing in return.

'I don't know,' Arnott answered quietly, 'He's lost a lot of blood, but he's tough, and if he makes it through the night, then he might have a chance of pulling through.'

Butch lowered his head. Tears welled up in his eyes.

Arnott sat with Butch for a while keeping vigil beside the bed where Sundance lay barely breathing, and Butch told him about Luther Greeley shooting his partner, and that he was worried that Greeley might still be in Buffalo and that he would come looking for them. He did not know that Greeley had been shot and killed by the sheriff.

Arnott scratched his chin and said thoughtfully, 'I'll ride into Buffalo in the morning and speak to some of the townspeople, and see if I can find out if Greeley is still in the town.'

Butch said, 'OK, but be careful' – and so Arnott left the room.

Left alone with his wounded partner, Butch stared at him despairingly. The Kid's face was deathly pale, his eyes firmly closed, and his chest rose and fell feebly. Butch spoke softly to him, imploring him to live. The Kid was tough, Butch knew this better than anyone, and he had seen him get through worse than this, but the terrible dread in his heart did not diminish, and tears began to spill from his eyes. He placed his head in his hands, and his shoulders shook as he silently wept.

*

Night drew on, and the bedroom became blanketed in darkness. Butch lifted his head and wiped his eyes on his sleeve. Arnott entered the room and lit the oil lamp, and told Butch that Tommy would be sleeping in his parents' bedroom. He then checked on Sundance's condition before looking closely at Butch. The outlaw looked shattered, and his eyes were red-rimmed.

Arnott squeezed Butch's shoulder in a gesture of comfort, and before leaving the room, glanced across at Sundance and said: 'Sundance is a fighter, he don't let nothing beat him – try talking to him, it might help bring him round. . . .' He closed the door, and through the dim, flickering glow of the oil lamp, Butch stared fearfully at The Kid, watching the weak rise and fall of his chest.

He spoke to Sundance several times, telling him in a trembling voice that he had to pull through. There was no response from The Kid, who lay as still as death and scarcely breathing. Tears welled up in Butch's eyes again. He began to think back to the time when he and Sundance had first met.

Arnott's words echoed in his mind: '. . . try talking to him . . . .' – and as Butch stared at Sundance through tear-filled eyes, he decided he would do this, would try talking to his partner, and would narrate to him the story of how they had first met.

Speaking out loud in a shaky voice, Butch began to tell the story of how he had first met Sundance, and of all the events leading up to their eventual partnership. Their friendship, and then later their partnership, began when they met as two young men, then going by the names of Leroy and Lonzo, in a saloon in the town of Green River, Wyoming.

CHAPTER 2

It was mid-afternoon in the railroad town of Green River, Wyoming, and the two young men trotting their horses down the dusty street were Robert Leroy Parker and Emmett Layne. The town was named after the Green River which flowed nearby, and the two men knew the town quite well. They were riding through it on their way to work at the ranch of Caleb Baxter, a friend of theirs. Baxter's ranch was located in a remote valley known as Browns Hole, and Leroy and Emmett had worked for him several times in the past two years.

They trotted past a general store, then pulled their horses to a stop at the hitch rail of a saloon. They dismounted and tied them to the hitch rail, brushed down their dust-streaked clothes, and pushed through the batwing doors. The saloon was a small, nondescript place, and Leroy and Emmett had visited it a few times in the past. It wasn't a particular favourite of theirs as the bartender and owner, Elias Mangold (who happened to be a friend of Caleb Baxter), was sometimes quite surly, but they had felt in need of a whiskey, and it was the first saloon along the street.

*

Robert Leroy Parker, who went by his second name of Leroy, was five feet eleven inches tall and twenty-two years old. He had a lean and wiry physique, light blond, wavy hair, and pleasant, attractive facial features. He had a bright charismatic smile, and vivid kingfisher-blue eyes. He had been raised in Circleville, Utah, and was the oldest of thirteen children. He was adventurous and friendly by nature.

Leroy's friend and partner, Emmett Layne, was a year older than Leroy and about the same height. He had reddish-brown hair, and was of a slim build.

The two men had first met when Leroy was fifteen years old, and Emmett's family had bought a homestead near to where Leroy's family lived in Circleville. They had quickly become friends, and two years later, left their homes together to look for work. Their first job was at the ranch of a nearby neighbour, Dan Marshall, and while working at Marshall's ranch, they had met a man named Mike Cassidy. Mike was in his late thirties, and he took a liking to Leroy and Emmett. He taught them a lot about ranching and shooting – and also about cattle rustling.

Mike was involved in rustling with two other ranch hands, and they often took Leroy and Emmett along with them; they would round up any unbranded cattle they found, put their own brand on them, then sell the beasts at market.

The ranch owner, Dan Marshall, was unaware of the rustling being committed by Mike and the other two ranch hands, but when he eventually heard rumours concerning their unlawful activities from some of his neighbouring ranchers, he decided to confront them. But Mike and the two ranch hands were warned by a friend that Marshall had heard about what they were doing, and they hastily left the ranch.

Leroy and Emmett did not take part in any more cattle rustling after Mike and the other two hands had left the ranch, but carried on with their lives as law-abiding ranch hands.

Nevertheless Leroy had greatly admired Mike, and he sometimes liked to give his name as Leroy Cassidy.

The saloon was fairly quiet, Leroy and Emmett fleetingly noticed as they pushed through the batwing doors, with only three of the six tables in the small room being used. Elias Mangold, the dour-looking bartender and owner, gave a brusque nod to Leroy and Emmett. He knew them from their previous visits to the saloon.

Four bewhiskered, mean-looking men were seated at a table near to the bar, idly playing cards and drinking whiskey. They were dressed like cattlemen. They looked up as Leroy and Emmett walked up to the bar, and their eyes flashed in recognition. They then lowered their heads.

Leroy and Emmett did not pay much attention to the four men. At the bar, and with his usual pleasant smile, Leroy ordered two whiskies from the sullen-looking bartender.

Sitting at another table further back from the bar, was a young man seemingly engrossed in reading a small leather-bound book; he was holding it up in front of his face, and his wide-brimmed hat was pulled down over his forehead. It was difficult to see his facial features, and only a few strands of sandy-coloured hair were visible on his forehead beneath the wide-brimmed hat. An empty whiskey glass was on the table in front of him.

Seated at a table at the back of the room were two men with stubbly grey beards. They wore shabby clothes and sat hunched up in their seats. Their eyes were closed, and they appeared to be asleep, or maybe drunk.

Leroy took some money from out of his pocket to pay Mangold, and asked the bartender if he wanted a drink. Leroy liked buying drinks for people – in general he liked helping folks out in some way if he could. His smile was friendly, and his cheery, kingfisher-blue eyes were compelling, and Elias Mangold very nearly cracked a smile before saying no.

Leroy then turned away from the bar and, casting his eyes casually around the room, and still smiling, asked the other men seated at the tables if he could buy them all a drink. Emmett smiled as he stood at the bar next to Leroy: it was typical of his warm-hearted friend to offer to buy everyone a drink.

The young man who was reading the book did not even lift his head, and the two men seated at the back of the room with the stubbly beards also did not respond. They had now started to snore. But the four mean-looking men sitting at the table closest to the bar began to grin. They lifted their heads, still grinning, to look at Leroy.

The friendly smile on Leroy's face dimmed a little as he realized who the four men were. Standing beside him, Emmett noticed the sudden change in his friend's attitude, and turned around from the bar. He felt a sense of dismay as he recognized the four bewhiskered men: they were from the Cottonwood ranch, a neighbouring ranch to Caleb Baxter on the eastern side. An area of rugged, steep and broken country separated the two ranch lands.

The owner of the Cottonwood ranch, Bart Jarvis, was not on friendly terms with Caleb Baxter, and had frequently tried to claim Baxter's cattle as his own. When Leroy and Emmett had worked for Baxter in the past they had witnessed a few hostile encounters between Caleb Baxter and the owner and ranch hands of the Cottonwood ranch.

One of the four Cottonwood men was of stocky build, with long and straggly dark brown hair and whiskers. He was Archie Burdett, foreman of the Cottonwood ranch, and he was a loud-mouthed braggart and troublemaker. The three men with Burdett were ranch hands – Seth Roebuck, Eli Slater and Bill Gooch – and were his usual companions. The four men had stopped at the saloon for a drink on the way back to their ranch after visiting some ladyfriends of theirs.

A sneer replaced the grin on Burdett's face, and his eyes glinted mockingly at Leroy and Emmett, who stood back against the bar. He said to his three grinning companions, 'Look who we've got here, boys, it's Caleb Baxter's friends, Parker and Layne. . . !'

Leroy relaxed back against the bar and began to smile easily at the four men. He sensed they wanted to stir up trouble, but they did not frighten him. Leroy was an easygoing young man who always tried to avoid violence and trouble, but he had a fearless nature. He could be tough when he had to be, and he wasn't afraid to stand up to anything or anyone. Emmett was no coward, either, and he was ready to take on the four Cottonwood men if he had to.

Burdett and his three friends laughed loudly and mirthlessly. The sneering Burdett then said to Leroy, 'I'm guessing that you two are on your way to work at Baxter's ranch again. . . !'

'What if we are?' Leroy asked coolly, still keeping his easy smile.

Burdett said menacingly to Leroy, 'The four of us ain't forgotten, Parker, that you and your friend, Layne, called us liars the last time that you were working for Baxter!'

Leroy still smiled. He said calmly to Burdett, 'You got a bad memory, Burdett, it weren't me or Emmett who called the four of you liars – it was Caleb Baxter.'

Leroy and Emmett remembered clearly the incident that Burdett was talking about. It had happened on Caleb Baxter's land. Archie Burdett, along with his three cohorts, Roebuck, Slater and Gooch, had been trying to herd away a bunch of unbranded calves from Baxter land, when Caleb, Leroy and Emmett, alerted by the bawling of the animals, had ridden up to them and challenged them about what they were doing.

Burdett and the three men with him had claimed that because the calves were unbranded they belonged to the Cottonwood ranch, and had somehow wandered on to Baxter land. Baxter had called the men liars and told them to get off his land.

Burdett and his three companions had then started to draw their guns, but Leroy and Emmett had drawn their own weapons faster, and ultimately, Burdett and his friends had ridden away cursing.

Archie Burdett was obviously still angry about the incident, and about being forced to back down by Leroy and Emmett. He pushed his chair back, scraping it on the wooden floor, and rose to his feet.

The young man reading the book at the table further back, lifted his eyes from the pages of his book, though no one noticed him doing it.

Burdett approached Leroy and Emmett. He stood in front of Leroy, only about a foot away from him. The easy smile stayed on Leroy's face, but Burdett said in a dangerous tone, 'Let's hear you call me a liar now.'

An uneasy atmosphere filled the room. The dour bartender, Elias Mangold, backed away from the bar, muttering something about not wanting any trouble. He had seen Burdett and his friends beat up men in his saloon on previous occasions. The two men with the stubbly grey beards sitting at the back of the room carried on snoring.

The young man with the book lifted his eyes up some more, and placed the book down on the table next to the empty glass. He then sat upright in his chair and pushed his hat up off his forehead to watch with interest the fraught scene at the bar.

Leroy said mildly, 'I never called you a liar before . . . but I reckon Caleb was right in what he said.' Leroy did not want a confrontation, but he knew that Burdett did, and that the man could not be reasoned with.

Burdett's hands were at his sides, but his fists had started to curl up. Meanwhile Emmett kept his eyes on the other three men still seated at the table – and sure enough, three more chairs scraped the floor of the saloon as Roebuck, Slater and Gooch rose to their feet, and began to move slowly but purposefully towards the bar.

While Emmett watched the three men as they moved towards them, Burdett suddenly brought up his fist and threw a punch at Leroy's belly. But Leroy swiftly caught the fist in his hand, and at the same time drove his knee forcefully into Burdett's groin. The man howled in pain and sank to the floor, clutching his groin.

Leroy did not see it, but a glint of curiosity appeared in the icy, steel-like, grey-blue eyes of the sandy-haired young man as he stared fixedly at Leroy Parker. He was impressed by Leroy's actions.

Roebuck, Slater and Gooch stood still for a second to gape open-mouthed at the wailing Burdett, then they bounded forwards at Leroy and Emmett. The two young men met them head on. Leroy ducked a swinging right blow from Seth Roebuck, and smashed his fist into the man's jaw, sending Roebuck crashing heavily to the floor.

Simultaneously, Emmett charged at Slater and Gooch as they leapt towards him: he drove his right shoulder into the chest of Eli Slater, knocking the man off his feet, then buried his fist into the stomach of Bill Gooch, following it up with a blow to his face. Gooch crashed over backwards, his head striking the wooden floor with a sickening thud.

Eli Slater had fallen awkwardly to the floor after being knocked off his feet by Emmett, but he suddenly sprang, clumsily but hastily, to his feet with his gun in his hand: before Leroy and Emmett could do anything, he aimed it at them and ordered them coldly to stand still and raise their hands.

Taken by surprise, Leroy and Emmett could do nothing but obey.

Slater's eyes were without pity, and it was chillingly obvious that he intended to kill the two men: he had pulled back the trigger of his gun ready to open fire. But suddenly he was grabbed from behind by the sandy-haired young man who had been reading the book.

The young man who intervened to save the lives of Leroy and Emmett was Harry Alonzo Longbaugh, who went by the name of Lonzo. He was twenty-two years old (although he looked younger), and he had been born in Mont Clare, Pennsylvania. He had left home at the age of fifteen to work on an uncle's ranch in Colorado. After leaving this he had worked at various other ranches around Colorado and Wyoming. He was skilled at breaking in and training horses; he was also very fast and accurate with a gun, a skill he tried to hide.

A little over seven months previously, Lonzo had been released from prison in the black hills town of Sundance, Wyoming. He had been imprisoned for stealing a horse and some food from a ranch where he had previously been employed. He had been dismissed from the ranch because there had been no more work for him to do, and he had been unable to find suitable work anywhere else. He had been forced to sell his horse for money to survive.

Finally, having no other option, he had sneaked back into the ranch where he had been last employed to steal a horse and some food. But he had been caught by some of the ranch hands and turned over to the law, and was sentenced to eighteen months in prison in the town of

Sundance. When his jail sentence had finished, Harry Alonzo Longbaugh came out of prison with a new name: he was now known as the Sundance Kid, a nickname given to him while he was in jail.

After leaving prison, Lonzo – under his new identity of the Sundance Kid – had become friendly with a couple of outlaws, who had involved him in a few gunfights; after one of these they had tried to pin the blame on him and get him arrested, and had deserted him. He had not killed any of his opponents in the shoot-outs, only wounded them, but he had gained a reputation for being fast with a gun – and ever since, he had tried to conceal the fact that he was known as the Sundance Kid from anyone he met. He always gave his name as Lonzo, as he didn't like having a reputation for his speed with a gun.

Lonzo swung Slater round to face him, and before Slater could open fire with the gun that he still held, or react in any way, rammed his bunched-up fist into the man's mid-section. Slater moaned and crumpled to the floor, barely conscious. His gun slipped from his weakened hand, and Lonzo kicked the weapon across the floor.

Leroy stared intently at the young man who had come to the aid of himself and Emmett, trying to weigh him up. The man was a stranger to them both, and had undoubtedly saved their lives.

Lonzo was tall – he touched the six-foot mark. He was dressed all in black – his pants, shirt and hat. His body was long and lean, but his frame was developing a strong musculature. His facial features, from what Leroy glimpsed of them, were youthful and tanned, but also well defined, and with more than a hint of impressive good looks. In the few seconds that Leroy was able to appraise Lonzo and busily scrutinize him, he sensed the quiet strength and fearlessness of the man – and to his inner delight, he also sensed that Lonzo had the same kind of adventurous spirit that he had.

Leroy started to speak – he was going to thank Lonzo for saving his own and Emmett's life – but he didn't get the chance, because, without a glance at anyone, Lonzo quickly turned, and avoiding stepping on the four Cottonwood men, strode across the floor and pushed through the doors, and stepped out into the dusty street.

Leroy felt a little disappointed as he stared after him. He would have liked to have spoken to the strangely reticent young man.

Elias Mangold, who had taken a few steps back from the bar when all the trouble had started, moved back up to the counter. He almost gave way to an amused smile as he glanced down at the scene in front of the bar. Archie Burdett was curled up practically into a ball on the floor; he was making a wailing sound. Seth Roebuck sat on the floor, rubbing his jaw; he looked dazed, and blood trickled through his fingers. Slater lay on his side, groaning and clutching his midsection; while Bill Gooch was lying on his back, out cold.

Mangold was pleased to see the four loud-mouthed intimidators being beaten for a change, and he poured out two fresh whiskies for Leroy and Emmett. The two men drank them up while keeping an eye on the four Cottonwood men.

Leroy's thoughts, though, were focused on the bold

young stranger who had saved the lives of his partner and himself, and he remarked thoughtfully to Emmett, 'That young man saved our lives – I wonder why he didn't hang around long enough for us to thank him?'

Mangold, having heard Leroy's words, said, 'I wouldn't worry about not thanking him, you'll be seeing him again soon enough. . . .'

Leroy shot him a look, and said 'What do you mean by that? Do you know who he is?'

'Sure, I know who he is,' Mangold answered, 'His name is Lonzo, and he sometimes comes in here for a drink when he picks up supplies in town for his boss. He works at the ranch of a mutual friend of ours, Caleb Baxter – and I think that you two are riding to Caleb's ranch to work for him again, aren't you?'

A slow smile spread across Leroy's face as he nodded to Mangold. It seemed as if he was destined to meet Lonzo again. He wasn't sure why the thought pleased him so much – but then he frowned, and said in a puzzled tone to Mangold: 'But why did he rush off like that? Why didn't he wait for us to ride with him to Caleb's ranch? He must have heard what Burdett said about me and Emmett being on our way to work for Caleb again. . . !'

'He heard all right,' Mangold replied, 'He don't miss nothing, but he ain't the friendly type – he's a loner and likes to keep to himself. . . .'

Mangold's words puzzled Leroy even more, and he said, 'Well, why then did he step in and save me and Emmett?'

Mangold shrugged, 'Who knows why he does anything? He's a strange one.'

26

Emmett suddenly grinned at his partner and said, 'It looks like you'll find it hard to work your magic on him.'

Leroy grinned back at him. They both knew that Emmett was referring to the special charm that Robert Leroy Parker possessed – the charm that sometimes compelled even total strangers to suddenly trust him.

The two men said farewell to Mangold and left the saloon, stepping around the Cottonwood ranch hands as they left. They mounted their horses and rode south towards Browns Hole and the ranch of Caleb Baxter.

CHAPTER 3

Leroy and Emmett camped overnight near a steep bank and under the shelter of some trees before continuing their ride to Browns Hole.

Leroy had a restless night. He found himself thinking about the mysterious Lonzo, and wondering if he had camped somewhere nearby. For some reason the man intrigued him a lot, and he wondered if, maybe, it was because he had sensed that they both had the same kind of adventurous spirit. Then, as he lay awake, his thoughts turned to someone else: a young lady named Amy Bassett. Amy was the girl he had promised to marry at only six years of age. She was intelligent and caring, and she had a natural beauty.

Amy's family had been neighbours of Leroy's family in Circleville, Utah. He had grown up with her, and had loved her for as long as he could remember, but he had left her, and his parents, brothers and sisters, when he was seventeen years of age because he wanted adventure. He did not want an ordinary, mundane life. Settling down and raising a family, and working at a hard and tedious job for long hours, was not for him.

Early the following morning, and even before the sun had started to appear over the horizon, Leroy and Emmett awoke, and after eating a meal consisting of a few strips of dried meat and some biscuits, they climbed on to their horses and continued riding on the trail that would take them to the mountain-ringed valley of Browns Hole. There were only a few trails through the mountains and steep canyons that led to Browns Hole, and they were difficult to traverse.

The next part of the trail that Leroy and Emmett would follow would take them through mountain passes, across creeks and streams, and then through the Red Creek Badlands before finally entering Red Creek Canyon; from there, the trail sloped steeply downwards into Browns Hole. The lush valley of Browns Hole was located part in the territories of Wyoming and Utah, and part in the state of Colorado. It was over fifty miles long and over fifteen miles wide, and was bordered by hills, canyons and mountains of various colours and vegetation. The Green River flowed through the valley.

Browns Hole had excellent grazing land and plentiful wildlife including deer, elk and wolves. Several homesteaders and ranchers had made the valley their home, and they had settled on both sides of the river.

Shortly before midday, Leroy and Emmett trotted out of Red Creek Canyon. They then had to ride for over two miles down a steep and gravelly trail before entering the valley.

After riding into Browns Hole, they rode for a few miles

through the tall grasses and vegetation of the valley, finally pulling their horses to a halt in a clearing where a small group of log buildings was situated near to the north bank of the river. The wooden buildings stood a few feet apart and were sheltered from behind by a range of hills. They were the properties of Jeremiah Baxter, the older brother of Caleb.

The sturdy log buildings were long and not too narrow, and constructed out of pine and spruce logs. There was a general store, an eating house, a saloon and a couple of log cabins with corrals attached. The general store and log cabins had been in the valley for a number of years, but the saloon and eating-house were fairly recent buildings. Jeremiah ran this small community with his wife, Dinah, his sons Levi, Warren and Sam, his daughter Annie, and some assistant workers.

Leroy and Emmett stepped inside the general store to buy some supplies and were warmly welcomed by Sam and Levi Baxter, who knew the two men quite well from the several times that they had worked on the ranch of their uncle, Caleb. After buying the supplies, Leroy and Emmett went into the eating-house for a meal. They were served by Annie, the daughter of Jeremiah and Dinah.

Annie had long, curly brown hair and hazel eyes. She was very attractive and had a sweet nature. She exchanged an affectionate smile with Emmett. Annie and Emmett had taken a strong liking to each other during the times that he had worked for Caleb, and they were pleased to see each other again.

Leroy and Emmett finished their meal and spent a few minutes talking to Annie before getting to their feet to leave the eating-house. Annie went outside with them, and while Leroy swung up into the saddle of his horse that was tied to the hitch rail alongside Emmett's, she stood talking quietly to Emmett. Leroy smiled as Emmett gave Annie a hesitant kiss on the cheek before mounting his horse.

There was a happy glow on Annie's face as she stood watching them ride away.

Caleb Baxter's ranch was located on the eastern border of Browns Hole in the state of Colorado, and it was late afternoon when Leroy and Emmett arrived there. It had taken them over two hours to ride through the valley to get to the ranch after leaving Annie.

They rode into the ranch grounds and looked around them. A few yards to their right were two corrals about ten feet apart. In the first one, nearest to them, they could see several horses milling around. In the second, which was smaller, Leroy and Emmett saw only one horse. It looked like a young mustang, and it had a saddle on its back. Three men were standing by the corral fence watching the horse. They had their backs to Leroy and Emmett, and the two friends glanced only briefly at the men, but they did notice that one of them looked like the ranch foreman, Deke Hogan.

Leroy and Emmett guessed that Hogan was probably breaking in the mustang. They knew it was one of the jobs that Hogan liked to do, but they also knew that the foreman could be brutal with the horses at times, and they felt an urge to ride over to the corral to watch how Hogan handled the young horse. However, first they would have to call in at the ranch house to let Caleb know they had arrived.

31

The ranch house stood across the yard from the corrals. It was a long, timber-framed, single-storey building with five rooms: a living room, kitchen and two bedrooms, while the fifth room was used as a library. Caleb loved reading, and he had built the fifth room on to the ranch house especially for his collection of books.

Other log buildings that stood to the right, left and rear of the ranch house were barns, stables and two bunkhouses. Rising up behind the ranch buildings was a series of low hills and mountains.

Leroy and Emmett rode on over to the ranch house. They dismounted and tied their horses to the hitch rail on the porch.

They had just stepped up on to the porch when they heard the loud neighing of a horse, and looked over at the corrals. Hogan was now inside the smaller corral with the mustang, and he was leading the young horse around by the reins. The mustang seemed very nervous, an indication that he must only recently have been introduced to accepting the saddle on his back and the feel of the bridle.

Leroy and Emmett stepped down from the porch and took a few steps nearer to the corral. Leroy, who loved horses and had a way with them, stared at the young mustang admiringly. The horse was golden tan in colour, and had a muscular body.

Hogan looked across at Leroy and Emmett with a dark scowl on his face. He wasn't happy to see them – in fact he was quite angry about the fact that they were going to be working at the ranch again. Caleb looked on Leroy too favourably for Hogan's liking.

Leroy and Emmett exchanged a knowing smile with

each other. In all the times they had worked at the Baxter ranch, they had never found Deke Hogan easy to deal with. Hogan was a hard worker, but he could behave in a very underhand and intimidating way – Leroy and Emmett had seen him deal roughly with some of the ranch hands in the past.

The two ranch hands leaning against the corral fence watching Hogan noticed the foreman's scowl, and turned round to look at Leroy and Emmett. A delighted smile sprang instantly to Leroy's face as he and Emmett recognized one of the ranch hands as the young man who had saved their lives in Green River, the puzzling and unfriendly Lonzo.

A flicker of recognition showed in Lonzo's grey-blue eyes as he looked at Leroy and Emmett, but he gave them no greeting, and ignoring Leroy's smile, turned his glance back to Hogan and the mustang. Leroy's smile died away, and he said rather sourly to Emmett, 'I guess now isn't a good time to thank him for saving our lives!'

Emmett could not help a sudden grin. Not many people could rile the easygoing Leroy Parker, but it looked as though Lonzo was going to be one of the few people who could, and he thought it would be interesting to see how things turned out between the amiable and cheerful Leroy, and the aloof Lonzo. Leroy had seen Emmett's grin, but before he could comment on it, Caleb Baxter came hurrying out of the ranch house to greet them.

Caleb was in his late forties, tall and sinewy in physique, with greying hair that was swept back off his forehead. He had a wife, Elizabeth, and two daughters, though both of his daughters were married and had moved away, and had little to do with their parents or the ranch. He was very firm with all his employees, but he was also a fair-minded man, and Leroy and Emmett liked him a lot.

Caleb shook hands with his two friends. He had been expecting them, and welcomed them by saying how pleased he was to have them work for him again. At his suggestion, the three men then walked the short distance across to the corral to watch Hogan and the mustang. Caleb did not know that Leroy and Emmett had already met Lonzo, and at the corral fence, he introduced them to both Lonzo and Marvin Kilbey, the other young ranch hand. Kilbey, a tall, fair-haired young man with pleasant blue eyes, smiled hello to them, but Lonzo only gave a non-committal grunt.

Leroy felt a rare rush of annoyance at Lonzo's attitude, and had to stop himself from uttering a very unpleasant remark. Lonzo turned his head away, but there was a glint of amusement in his eyes. He had noticed how Leroy had suppressed his sudden flare of irritation.

Lonzo hated to admit it to himself, but Leroy Parker intrigued him, and had done so ever since he had seen him drive his knee into Archie Burdett's groin. Back then in the saloon in Green River, when Leroy had scrutinized him so keenly, Lonzo had sensed in Leroy an adventurous spirit and a fearlessness that matched his own.

Lonzo, however, had no wish to get friendly with Leroy or anyone else – he did not trust people, and he did not want anyone to know or guess that he also went by the name of the Sundance Kid.

While Caleb and the other men watched him, Hogan

stopped leading the young mustang around the corral as he was now thinking of jumping up into the saddle to try and ride it. Before attempting to do this, he called out to Marvin Kilbey to open the corral gate – once he had got up into the saddle and had the horse under sufficient control, then he intended to ride it out of the ranch grounds and over the range land for a few miles to show it who was the boss.

Deke Hogan was a daunting figure of a man. He was over six foot tall and burly, with well developed muscles. He had black hair, and his dark eyes always seemed to emit a menacing gleam.

Hogan was aware that his boss, Caleb Baxter, was watching as he leapt up into the mustang's saddle, and he wanted to make a good impression. Hogan liked to be the one at Baxter's ranch to break in the young and spirited horses, and it infuriated him that ever since Lonzo had turned up at the ranch looking for work about six months ago, and had shown such prowess with horses, Caleb had given a lot of the horse breaking and training jobs to him. He was further angered by the fact that Leroy Parker, who also had a special way with horses, had just arrived at the ranch with his partner, Emmett Layne, to work for Baxter again.

The instant the mustang felt Hogan in the saddle, its muscles bunched and it began to buck as it tried frantically to unseat Hogan from its back, leaping and twisting with speed around the corral, and trying to throw himself over backwards as Hogan tried desperately to keep his seat.

Leroy watched intently along with the other men at the corral fence. Then the mustang suddenly gave a violent pitch forwards, and Hogan fell from the saddle into the dirt. The horse stood panting. Its sides were heaving, and its eyes were darting everywhere.

Hogan had landed hard, but he was soon up on his feet. His face was red with fury as he made a grab for the horse's bridle. He also bunched up his fist, and the men who were leaning against the corral fence watching, all believed that Hogan was going to throw a punch at the horse.

Leroy yelled out, 'No, Deke!'

But Hogan didn't get the chance to hit the horse, because it suddenly plunged into a run, the bridle was torn from Hogan's hands, and in a flurry of hoofs it charged towards the open corral gate.

Leroy immediately darted towards the open gate and reached it just as the mustang was galloping up to it. He leapt for its head and grabbed hold of the reins. The horse snorted wildly, and instantly started kicking out and trying to rear up, but Leroy held tight on to the reins. His breath came in gasps as he struggled to keep the animal from rearing up while avoiding the flaying hoofs.

There was a sudden rush of movement on the other side of the horse, and out of the corner of his eye, Leroy saw to his dismay that Deke Hogan was running up to try and grab the reins on the opposite side. Someone else, however, had the same idea as Hogan, and he pushed in front of the foreman, almost sending him tumbling over.

It was Harry Alonzo Longbaugh, the young man from Pennsylvania, who caught hold of the mustang's reins on the opposite side to Leroy, and Leroy was glad that it was Lonzo who had hold of the reins and not the brutish Deke Hogan.

Caleb, Emmett and Marvin Kilbey were running up close behind Lonzo. The combined strength of Leroy and Lonzo gripping the reins kept the horse from rearing up, but they struggled to keep their footing, and finally Leroy stumbled and fell. He rolled over in the dirt, then sat in the dust and watched as Lonzo grabbed hold of the saddle horn and vaulted into the mustang's saddle.

Having another rider on its back immediately caused the mustang to explode into renewed and frantic bucking. Dust swirled around the plunging horse and the onlookers as Lonzo was jerked up and down and from side to side in the saddle.

Emmett went over to help Leroy to his feet. Leroy dusted himself down. He felt a bit disgruntled as he watched the struggle between Lonzo and the mustang. The horse was leaping and twisting with vigour and speed to try and unseat the man in the saddle, but by using the reins skilfully, and with little use of the spurs, Lonzo prevented the horse from getting its head up and trying to rear over backwards.

Deke Hogan tried to hide his glower of fury. He was mindful of how close his boss stood to him, and he did not want Caleb to see his anger. All he could do was stand and watch Lonzo and the horse. He felt that not only had he been beaten by the mustang, but by Leroy and Lonzo as well. And it didn't help his mood when Caleb remarked with a smile to no one in particular, 'Lonzo sure has a way with horses, and a lot of guts!'

Caleb then turned to look at Leroy who stood to one side of him with Emmett, and said, 'In fact, he reminds me of you.' Leroy wasn't sure if he should consider that remark to be a compliment or not, but as he watched Lonzo being jolted around on the mustang's back, he could not help but feel some admiration for the man. Emmett noticed the admiration in Leroy's eyes and smiled, because even though Leroy might not have been aware of it yet, Emmett knew that his partner felt a certain kinship with Lonzo.

The struggle between the horse and the man continued for a few more minutes, and in the glimpses that he caught of Lonzo's eyes, Leroy saw a steel-like determination – and he got the feeling that Lonzo was not a man who liked to lose at anything. Then suddenly the horse stopped its leaping and twisting, and lunged into a run.

Leroy, Emmett and the other men watched as the young mustang, with Lonzo still on its back, charged away from the corral, out of the ranch yard, and along the trail that led north away from the ranch. The horse tried to swerve off the trail into the trees and brush a couple of times, but Lonzo swung him back, and it was obvious to those watching that Lonzo had control of the horse.

The two bunkhouses at the ranch slept up to six men, but could accommodate more if necessary. Cook shacks were attached to each bunkhouse. Caleb had a resident cook, but the ranch hands could do their own cooking if they wanted to. The beds were narrow and timber framed with straw mattresses, arranged in rows of three up against opposite walls. The ranch foreman, Deke Hogan, had a cabin to himself.

Leroy and Emmett took their few belongings into the bunkhouse they would be sharing with Lonzo and Marvin

Kilbey; they were sorting through their bits and pieces when Kilbey joined them and started chatting to them about the jobs that needed doing on the ranch. During the conversation, Leroy asked him what it was like to work with Lonzo.

Kilbey thought for a moment, then said, 'Lonzo is a good worker, but he ain't the easiest man to get along with – he don't believe in having a friendly chat with anyone, or in making friends.'

Leroy sighed, 'That's just what I figured. . . .'

Kilbey gave a sudden laugh, 'I'm real glad you two will be sharing the bunkhouse with us – at least now I've got someone to talk to!'

Leroy and Emmett laughed. Five minutes later, Leroy left Emmett and Kilbey talking, and went back outside. He intended to wait near to the corral for the return of Lonzo and the mustang. He saw Deke Hogan and Caleb talking together near to the empty corral and started to make his way towards them, but as he walked closer to them, they began to walk away. He smiled as he heard Caleb saying to Hogan that he did not want him to be too brutal when breaking in the horses. Caleb had evidently not approved of Hogan trying to hit the mustang.

Leroy leaned against the corral fence and cast his eyes over the skyline for some sign of Lonzo and the horse. No matter how long he had to wait, he was *determined* to speak to Lonzo. He still wanted to thank him for saving his life.

He had been waiting only about two or three minutes when Lonzo and the golden-tan mustang came into view from the north. The mustang was galloping fast and a little erratically along the trail leading to the ranch yard and buildings, but Leroy knew that Lonzo had him under control. He suddenly smiled: Lonzo had left some spirit in the horse, and he liked that.

Lonzo slowed the horse down as he entered the ranch yard and rode towards where Leroy waited by the corral. He pulled the horse to a stop, and although he must have seen Leroy, he did not even look at him as he dismounted and led the mustang back into the corral, closing the gate behind them. Without so much as a glance in Leroy's direction, Lonzo started to take off the saddle and bridle from the horse. The mustang whinnied nervously, but Lonzo calmed it down by talking softly to it and gently rubbing his hand over its back.

Leroy watched Lonzo closely. He could usually judge people quite well, and he sensed that Lonzo was not as unfriendly and unfeeling as he liked people to think he was. He called out cheerily: 'Hey . . . you left that saloon in Green River before me and Emmett could thank you for saving our lives!'

A minute or two passed by before Lonzo finally lifted his attention from the horse and looked at Leroy. A pair of impassive and steel-like grey-blue eyes centred on Leroy, his steady gaze seeming to penetrate into the very soul of the young man. He then turned his attention back to the horse, gently rubbing its back again, and muttered, without looking at Leroy, 'It was nothing personal, I just ain't got no liking for bullies and bigmouths like Archie Burdett, or uneven odds. . . .'

His accent had not sounded southern, but it was hard for Leroy to make it out because Lonzo's voice was so low.

'I guess that's lucky for me and Emmett,' Leroy smiled.

40

Lonzo did not say anything. He carried on rubbing the mustang's back, and his attitude showed that he clearly wanted to be left alone.

Leroy's intuition was telling him that Lonzo was as outspoken as he was fearless and adventurous, and that it would be wise to leave him alone – but he wasn't going anywhere, and instead he asked, 'Is Lonzo your first name or your last?'

Lonzo rubbed over the horse a couple more times, then walked over to the corral gate, opened it and stepped out. He stood a few feet away from Leroy as he closed the gate. In fact he already felt an affinity with Leroy Parker that annoyed him, one he didn't want, and he was now further annoyed by Leroy's obvious determination to have a conversation with him.

For a moment, Leroy thought that Lonzo was going to ignore his question and just walk away, but he did not – instead he looked at Leroy and said curtly, 'Why is that of any interest to you, Parker?' His voice was low, yet strong and confident at the same time, and clear enough for Leroy to detect the hint of an eastern accent.

'We'll be working together,' Leroy replied with a friendly smile, trying to ignore Lonzo's curtness, 'And me and Emmett will be sharing the bunkhouse with you and Marvin, so I'd like to call you by your first name – it's more friendly that way, don't you think?'

At that moment Emmett stepped out of the bunkhouse looking for his partner, and as he started to walk towards Leroy and Lonzo, he heard the rest of their conversation. Lonzo said coldly to Leroy, 'Like you said, we'll be *working* together, and as far as I'm concerned, we're here to work,

41

not to become friends.'

Leroy grinned, and burst out: '*By jingo*! You believe in plain speaking, don't you?'

Lonzo seemed on the point of saying something else, but instead he glanced towards Emmett who was walking up to them, and then strode away in the direction of one of the stables. Emmett said to Leroy with a grin as he reached him, 'It don't look like your charm is working on him yet!'

Leroy smiled, and said 'Give it time!' – and he meant it.

Emmett laughed, and the two friends began to walk back to the bunkhouse together. They chatted merrily as they walked.

They failed to see Lonzo halt in his purposeful stride towards the stable to glance back at them, and they did not see the brief touch of warmth that flashed in his usually impassive eyes.

CHAPTER 4

Caleb Baxter owned a lot of land and several hundred head of cattle. He had line cabins spaced out across his range land for the ranch hands to live in while they were looking after the cattle.

The next few days were busy ones for Leroy and Emmett. They spent most of the time in the saddle, and their jobs included moving the cattle on to better grazing land, helping them out of mud holes when they got stuck, and keeping a lookout for predators, mainly cougars and bears, to prevent them from coming too close to the cattle.

They were usually too exhausted at night to do anything but rest, and even though he shared their bunkhouse, they saw little of Lonzo. He was awake and out with Kilbey, riding a different range to them, before they woke up. He did eat with them sometimes in the evenings, but following that, he would always go off somewhere on his own. Leroy often tried to engage him in conversation, but all he got out of him were a few gruff remarks.

Leroy and Emmett had been working on the ranch for

about a month, when, on one particularly warm evening after they had eaten a late dinner, Leroy found it too warm to sit in the bunkhouse, and he took a walk to Caleb's library room. Lonzo had gone off on his own as usual, and Kilbey and Emmett were playing cards while taking a swig of whiskey from a bottle that Kilbey kept hidden.

Leroy had always loved reading, but he had not had the chance to visit Caleb's library until now. The library room had a separate outside door that could be used by anyone on the ranch who wanted to go in to read, so Leroy did not have to walk through the ranch house to gain entrance to it. It had just one small window, and otherwise the walls were lined with shelves for the large number of books that Caleb had bought or acquired. These were by various authors such as Jules Verne, Mark Twain and Charles Dickens.

The room was lit by two large oil lamps that hung down from the ceiling, and there were a couple of tables and chairs in the centre – and to Leroy's surprise, sitting at one of the tables and apparently absorbed in reading a book, was Lonzo. Leroy's mind flashed back for a second to the saloon in Green River and the first time that he had set eyes on Lonzo. The young man had been sitting at a table in the saloon reading a book, and he seemed to be reading the same small, leather-bound book now (this was not one of Caleb's books, but his own). Lonzo glanced up at Leroy with no expression on his face.

'So,' Leroy said with his most charming smile, 'This is where you disappear to most evenings! I was beginning to think that you had a young lady hidden somewhere. . . !'

Lonzo said nothing. He dropped his eyes back down to

the pages of his book.

'What are you reading?' Leroy asked, still smiling. He stepped up closer to Lonzo, and tried to see what the title of the book was.

'I came here to *read*, not to talk,' Lonzo muttered without lifting his eyes from his book. Leroy again thought he heard the trace of an eastern twang in Lonzo's voice, and he also caught a glimpse of the title on the book cover. It was a Jules Verne novel entitled *From the Earth to the Moon.*

'I like Jules Verne too,' Leroy said cheerily.

Lonzo looked up at him again with annoyance showing in his eyes, and Leroy began to feel worried that he might just get up and walk out, so he quickly moved away from him and grabbed a book off the shelf to read. He sat down at the other table in the room and commenced reading. Lonzo looked back down at his book, but not before a faint smile had touched his face.

Leroy had not noticed Lonzo's smile, nor did he know that he had already impressed the young man from Pennsylvania, in much the same way that he had been equally impressed and intrigued by Lonzo.

After that night, there would be many more evenings that Leroy and Lonzo spent together reading in the library room. There wasn't much conversation between the pair, but at least Lonzo appeared to accept Leroy's presence in the room.

Two weeks later, and towards the end of a very warm afternoon, Leroy and Emmett rode into the ranch yard and dismounted near to one of the corrals. They had been busy out on the range since dawn, and were feeling weary – they could feel their bones aching with tiredness as they tended to their horses and let them loose in the corral. Carrying their saddles, they walked towards the bunkhouse; they felt in need of some rest and possibly sleep – but their attention was unexpectedly drawn to something else.

They heard shouts, and a few feet to the left of the bunkhouse they saw a group of five men standing in an untidy sort of circle watching something. Deke Hogan was one of the men in the circle. Feeling curious, and temporarily forgetting their weariness, Leroy and Emmett walked up to join the disorderly circle of men to see what was going on.

A wrestling match of sorts was taking place, and the two men wrestling each other were Marvin Kilbey and Lonzo.

When they had some free time, the ranch hands liked to amuse themselves by taking part in a few friendly sports, and wrestling was one of these. Leroy sighed, and remarked to Emmett that Lonzo might not want to make friends with anyone, but he apparently didn't mind taking part in a friendly wrestling match with other ranch workers.

Emmett smiled and said, 'Perhaps he likes a challenge.'

The ranch hands usually made up their own rules for all their sports contests, and the rules for this wrestling match were, that once one of the contestants had been thrown or forced to the ground in some way by his opponent, then the match was over.

Lonzo's youthful face was set in determination. Although the contest was a friendly one, he wanted to win:

losing was out of the question for Harry Alonzo Longbaugh, alias the Sundance Kid. When growing up along the canals in Pennsylvania, he had quickly learned how to wrestle and fight with the local bullies. He hadn't always won the fights, but he had never liked the taste of losing, and had grown up into a proud, stubborn and fearless young man who loved challenges and adventure.

As Leroy, Emmett and the other men in the circle stood watching, the contest between Lonzo and Kilbey did not last for much longer. The two men were gripping each other by the upper arms, and kicking out with their legs in an attempt to trip each other up. This went on for about a minute, and then a faint smile seemed suddenly to touch Lonzo's face – a smile that Leroy noticed – and in one incredibly fast movement, he pulled down on Kilbey's right arm, pushed hard on his left shoulder, and swept his foot round his ankles, hooking the ranch-hand's right leg and sending him off balance. Lonzo then pulled down harder on his opponent's right arm – and Marvin Kilbey fell to the ground.

At the same instant that Kilbey hit the ground, Lonzo's eyes focused for a second on Leroy and Emmett – but he did not acknowledge them, and then his eyes turned swiftly away as though he had not seen them.

Leroy felt a deep inward flush of irritation at Lonzo's rather insulting behaviour towards himself and Emmett, but after watching him in action in the wrestling contest with Kilbey, and witnessing his faint smile, he also felt that he knew a lot more about his character. He realized that not only was Lonzo a man who hated to let anything beat him, but that Emmett was right when he had said that Lonzo also loved a challenge.

Lonzo went on to win the next two wrestling contests against ranch hands who stepped out of the circle to challenge him. Only two young ranch workers were left in the group of onlookers who wanted to challenge him, but before either of them could do so, Deke Hogan took a step forwards to face Lonzo and said firmly, 'I'm next' – and the friendly mood of the contest straightaway changed.

Tension suddenly hung in the air. The wrestling contest was only meant to be between the young ranch hands, and Hogan was only supposed to be there as an interested spectator. But he was watching in the hope of seeing Lonzo lose: he was still angry with him over the episode with the mustang – he felt that the young man had shamed him in front of his boss – but now, Lonzo had not yet lost a contest, and it seemed unlikely that he would, and Hogan wanted to change that.

There was a smirk on Hogan's face as he stood in front of Lonzo, and the habitual, menacing gleam in his eyes appeared to be more prominent. His mighty frame seemed to dwarf the young Lonzo. There was no trace of fear in Lonzo's impassive grey-blue eyes as he gave a casual nod to his challenger. He would not back down: Hogan knew it, and Leroy and Emmett knew it.

Concern suddenly sprang into Leroy's eyes, and Emmett was not surprised when his partner abruptly dropped the saddle that he had been holding and rushed forwards to say to Hogan in a light but firm tone, 'This is hardly fair, Deke, Lonzo is just a boy compared to you, pick on someone your own size!'

Leroy knew that Hogan was trying to punish Lonzo because of what had happened with the mustang. He also knew that Lonzo would not thank him for interfering.

Hogan turned angrily on Leroy, 'Shut your mouth, Parker,' he snarled, 'or I'll wrestle you instead!'

Hogan had moved up close to Leroy and was looking down on him as though daring him to wrestle with him. Emmett frowned anxiously, but before Leroy could respond to what Hogan had said, Lonzo darted forwards and shoved him back out of the way.

'Stay out of this, Parker!' Lonzo snapped. 'No one asked you to interfere, this is between Hogan and me!'

Leroy reluctantly stayed back, and as he looked at Emmett, there was no mistaking the worry in his eyes.

Emmett felt puzzled at Lonzo's reason for shoving Leroy back. Was Lonzo concerned about Hogan's threat to wrestle Leroy, and Leroy getting hurt? Or was he worried that it would look as if he were backing down to Hogan by letting Leroy wrestle the man in his place? Emmett concluded it was the latter, that Lonzo did not want it to look as if he were backing down to Hogan – but in fact he was right on both counts.

Lonzo pushed Leroy back out of the way partly because his pride and stubbornness would never allow him to let anyone else wrestle Hogan in his place, and partly because (if he allowed himself to admit it) he was indeed concerned that Leroy would be hurt.

Hogan and Lonzo began their grappling, and Hogan quickly had a tight grip on Lonzo. He had hold of the young man by the thighs and was trying to lift him off his feet, and once he had Lonzo off his feet, he would then throw him to the ground.

Lonzo pushed down on Hogan's arms in a desperate effort to keep his feet on the ground. But Hogan squeezed on Lonzo's thighs more and more tightly as he tried to lift him – and he was grinning, as though he was confident he was going to win the contest easily.

Lonzo kept pushing back on Hogan's arms, and tried to kick out at him. Sweat trickled down his face. He was in pain, and only his determination was keeping him on his feet. Leroy wanted to run forwards to try and stop the contest, but he stayed where he was, as he didn't want to cause any more upset to Lonzo's fierce pride.

The minutes passed by, and Lonzo could not break Hogan's strong grip on his thighs, and his feet were beginning to slide. Hogan knew this, and his grin widened as he finally succeeded in lifting Lonzo a few inches off the ground. But somehow, either by sheer willpower or brute force, Lonzo pressed strongly down on Hogan's arms and regained his footing, but very shakily.

Hogan howled in rage, and forcefully flung Lonzo to one side. Inevitably Lonzo lost his footing and began to fall – but as he fell, he grabbed hold of Hogan's arm and pulled down hard on it with surprising and remarkable strength, and his unexpected action caused Hogan to lose his balance and fall forwards on to his face in the dust.

Leroy smiled at Emmett, and there was both relief and admiration in his smile. Marvin Kilbey and the other four ranch hands who were watching also had huge smiles on their faces. Hogan was not liked by any of the workers on Baxter's ranch as he intimidated them all too much.

Hogan raised his head up out of the dirt, and angrily saw the smiles of the men looking down on him – then he looked across at Lonzo, who was lying on his back just to the side of him.

Lonzo lay unmoving, but his eyes were open. The back of his head had struck the ground hard when he fell, and he felt a little faint. His thighs were throbbing with pain from Hogan's punishing hold, and for a second or two he had to lie still.

A sudden, murderous fury flared up inside Hogan as he looked at Lonzo. The young ranch hand had shamed him again. His fist closed around a large rock on the ground near to him, and with an angry roar he got to his knees and lunged at the motionless Lonzo with the rock – but before he could smash it down on Lonzo's head, his hand was grabbed from behind in a grip of steel by Leroy Parker.

Leroy's usually pleasant kingfisher-blue eyes were like ice. His voice was quite cold as he said to Hogan, 'Don't do it, Deke, this is supposed to be a friendly wrestling contest between the young ranch hands, and you wouldn't want to kill someone in a friendly contest that you weren't supposed to be taking part in, would you?'

Hogan's murderous fury was still raging through him, and his face was crimson with rage as he twisted his head to stare furiously into Leroy's face.

'I'm gonna kill you, Parker!' he growled out, and went to pull his hand free of Leroy's grip and leap to his feet to grab hold of him – but as he did so he caught sight of Caleb Baxter in the distance staring curiously at them all, then starting to walk over to them.

51

Cursing, Hogan made an effort to control the intensity of his raging anger, and with Leroy still gripping his hand, he opened his fingers and let the rock fall harmlessly to the ground. Leroy let go of his hand, and Hogan stood up. The ranch foreman said angrily through clenched teeth to Leroy, 'You'd better stop pushing your luck, Parker – being a favourite of Baxter's won't always save you!'

Hogan then roughly pushed past Leroy and the on-looking ranch hands, and strode off to meet Caleb halfway as his boss walked towards the group. He took Caleb's arm, and carefully steered him away from Leroy and the other ranch hands, saying jovially, 'Me and the boys were just taking part in a bit of friendly wrestling. . . .'

Leroy and Emmett went over to Lonzo, and Kilbey and the other ranch hands followed after Hogan and Caleb.

Leroy reached down to help Lonzo to his feet, but Lonzo brushed aside his help, and struggled awkwardly and painfully to his feet himself. He stood a little shakily, and rubbed the back of his head, which was grazed and bleeding.

'Are you OK?' Leroy asked.

Lonzo was not in a grateful mood. He looked at Leroy with angry eyes, and said sharply, 'You didn't have to inter-fere, Parker, I don't need your help or anyone else's!'

Leroy grinned genially, 'Yeah,' he said, 'You do defi-nitely believe in plain speaking – but I owed you that!'

'You owed me nothing!' Lonzo kept his sharp tone, 'Just stay out of my business in future, I don't want any more help from you, and don't expect any thanks!'

Leroy shrugged, 'Well, don't think of it as help, just think of it as a kind of favour from me to you.'

'To hell with you and your favours!' Lonzo snapped, and began to walk rather unsteadily away and towards the bunkhouse.

Emmett said to Leroy with a slight grin, 'I don't think your charm has won him over yet!'

Leroy felt a sudden feeling of exasperation at Lonzo's attitude as he looked at Emmett, and he said almost angrily 'That Lonzo has to be the most unfriendly, stubborn and arrogant man I have ever met!'

To Leroy's surprise, Emmett laughed and said, 'But that doesn't stop you from liking him!'

For a moment, Leroy just stared at Emmett in astonishment, '*Like hell I do*!' he finally burst out.

Emmett only laughed again. He knew that although his partner hotly denied it, Leroy felt an unexplainable liking for Lonzo.

As Leroy stood staring at him, Emmett picked up Leroy's saddle from where he had dropped it. He handed it to his partner, saying, 'We've been up since dawn and we're tired, so let's take these saddles into the bunkhouse, and get something to eat before we get some sleep . . .' and then he grinned, and added, 'That's if you don't mind being in the same place as Lonzo!'

CHAPTER 5

Over a week had passed since the wrestling contest, and Leroy and Emmett were out riding over the northern range of Caleb's ranch land. Grassy pastures, scrubland and low hills interspersed the northern range. A fiery sun blazed down on them, and both men were feeling the heat. After herding a bunch of cattle on to better grazing land, Leroy and Emmett dismounted and sat down amongst some rocks at the base of a low hill, known as Creek Hill by Caleb Baxter and his ranch hands.

They had given the hill its name because a wide creek strewn with pebbles wound its way across the range land a few feet away from where Leroy and Emmett were sitting in the rocks. Feeling tired from the heat of the sun, they began to close their eyes and doze off. But they had only been dozing for about five minutes when they were abruptly brought back to awareness by the drumming of hoofbeats. They opened their eyes and slowly stood up.

They felt rather sluggish as they stepped out of the rocks and looked round. To their right they saw two riders cantering through the grass and bushes, heading roughly towards them. They were still about a hundred yards away, but as they got closer, Emmett became very excited as he realized who they were. One of them was Annie Baxter, the daughter of Caleb's brother, Jeremiah, and the girl he felt increasingly attracted to. The other rider was Annie's friend, Maria Powell. Maria's family had their homestead in the valley, and Maria would sometimes help Annie in the eating house.

Emmett's face was beaming with joy as he hurried forwards to shout out to the two ladies. He wasn't sure if they had seen him and Leroy, but they heard him shout, looked over and then rode towards him. Annie was smiling as she and Maria reined in their horses close to where Emmett was standing. Both young ladies were dressed in riding skirts and plaid cotton blouses.

Emmett helped Annie down from her horse, and they both stood smiling fondly at each other as Leroy approached them. Leroy went over to Maria to help her dismount, but she declined his help and got down from her horse by herself. She was an independent kind of woman. She had long, black wavy hair and blue eyes, and was as good-looking as Annie, though not as demure or as fond of household tasks. Annie was quite happy doing household chores such as sewing and baking, and although Maria sometimes liked to help her with the cooking in the eating house, she much preferred being with horses and looking after livestock.

Emmett and Annie stood smiling affectionately at each other for another moment, then he asked her why she and Maria were out riding over the northern range of Caleb's ranch lands. He secretly hoped she had been looking for him.

Annie told Emmett that her parents had asked her and Maria to ride over to Caleb's ranch house with a message from them.

A rosy glow seemed to touch Annie's cheeks as Emmett still smiled lovingly at her. She continued talking and said, 'My parents are holding a dance at the eating house in four days' time, and they asked us to ride over to see Uncle Caleb and to invite him and anyone who works for him to the dance . . .' and she added almost coyly, 'Uncle Caleb told us that you two were out here on the northern range. . . .'

Dances were held regularly at Browns Hole for all and any occasion, and almost everyone in the valley was invited. Emmett took hold of Annie's arm after she had finished speaking, and the two of them began to walk away together. They obviously wanted to be alone with each other for a little while.

Smiling to himself at Emmett's happiness, Leroy sat down in the rocks again. Maria sat down beside him, and although she kept her glance away from him, he noticed a slightly troubled look appear on her face. Not many people would have noticed it, but Leroy was very perceptive, especially to other people's troubles.

'Is anything wrong?' he asked her.

Maria mumbled something about not wanting to talk about it. She had known Leroy for nearly two years, and she knew him to be a very friendly and helpful person, but she was reluctant to talk to him about what was troubling her.

Leroy said gently, 'Tell me what's wrong, and maybe I can help?'

He genuinely wanted to help, and this was obvious in his voice.

Maria looked at him: she found it hard to resist his charm, and the look in his eyes compelled her to trust him, but she felt a little embarrassed about what was worrying her. She had to look away from him as she said rather hesitantly, 'It's the dance at the eating house to celebrate Annie's mother's birthday. . . .' She broke off and didn't say anything else.

'What about the dance?' Leroy asked quietly.

Maria still looked away from him as she said, 'I feel like I'm letting Annie down if I don't go, but I ain't any good at dancing. . . .' she stopped speaking, and turned to look at him a little sheepishly, as though wondering if he would laugh at her – but he didn't, and she continued, 'I ain't got no sense of timing, I can never dance to the music's rhythm . . . at the last dance that I went to in the valley . . .' her voice dropped low, 'Most folks laughed at me. . . .'

Leroy had a sensitive side to his nature, and even though, on the outside, Maria appeared to be a strong woman who never let anything worry her, he could understand how it would upset her to be laughed at. He felt like giving her a hug to comfort her, but stopped himself in time. He knew that Maria was not the kind of girl who liked a fuss.

'Can't Annie help you with your dancing?' he asked.

'She has tried,' Maria sighed, 'And I don't want to let her down by not going to the dance, but I don't want to be laughed at again. . . .'

Leroy tried to think of something he could do to help her. He smiled happily as an idea came to him.

'I know a few dances,' he told her cheerily, 'I can help you learn to do the steps in time to the music!'

He was not a great dancer, but he knew most of the basic steps. He stood up and lightly pulled Maria to her feet, 'And I'll start helping you right now!'

Maria began to protest, but he took her arm and led her away from the rocks and on to a patch of fairly smooth ground just in front of them; then he drew her into his arms and started to do a few waltz steps with her. He hummed out the tunes while dancing with her.

She was very awkward on her feet, Leroy soon discovered as he danced with her, and she had been right about having no sense of timing, but he smiled encouragingly and hummed out the tunes as they danced.

After doing the waltz with her, Leroy danced her through some steps to the polka, and then to some square dances that he knew – but Maria still could not get any sense of timing, and eventually, after treading all over Leroy's feet, she pulled away from him, and sat back down in the rocks, looking very dejected.

Leroy tried to cheer her up, saying, 'I've danced with worse dancers than you, honestly I have. . . .'

Maria refused to look at him.

Emmett and Annie came back to join them just as Leroy was trying to persuade Maria to dance with him again, and the three of them talked her into having another try. Leroy and Emmett both danced with her in turn, and they whistled and hummed the tunes as they danced, but she still had trouble dancing the steps in time to the music.

Finally she stepped away from the two men, and said with a slight tremor in her voice, 'It's no use, I'll never get the timing of the steps right, I'm always going to look like a clumsy fool when I'm dancing, so I'll just stay away from the dance. . . .'

Annie went up to her and gave her a hug, and murmured some words of comfort. Leroy almost said to Maria that most folks at the dance would be too busy drinking and enjoying themselves to notice what she was doing, but he changed his mind, and instead tried to think of another way to help her.

He smiled, and his eyes twinkled with enthusiasm as an idea came to him. He called out happily to Maria, 'You won't have to stay away from the dance. . . .'

He looked from Emmett to Annie with eagerness still shining in his eyes, and said, 'If we can get someone to play the dance music for us while we three do the dance steps with Maria, I think it'll help her to get more of a sense of rhythm.'

Maria's face brightened for a moment, but then she pointed out that the dance was in four days' time.

'That's more than enough time,' Leroy assured her with a smile, 'Now all we have to do is find someone who can play the fiddle or some other musical instrument.'

Leroy could play the harmonica reasonably well, and he suggested to the others that he played the harmonica while Emmett danced with Maria if no one else could be found to play the music. Emmett, Annie and Maria did not look too impressed by his suggestion. They had heard Leroy play the harmonica on previous occasions, and he didn't always get the notes right.

Leroy saw their doubting faces – it was obvious they had little faith in his harmonica playing. 'Well, OK,' he said, then asked the girls, 'Do you two know of anyone in the valley we could ask to play the dance music for us?'

The two girls were quiet for a few minutes as they tried to think of someone in Browns Hole who played the fiddle or banjo. Then they both suddenly smiled at the same time as they remembered something, but it was Annie who burst out excitedly to Leroy, 'I think I *do* know someone! There's a man who works here on Uncle Caleb's ranch who plays the fiddle, he's played for the diners in our eating-house a few times, and I'm sure you must know him – he's called Lonzo and he's very good. . . .'

Leroy's face changed at her words, and Emmett laughed.

The sky was darkening, and the daytime heat had cooled a little as Lonzo sat alone reading in the library room at Caleb's ranch house. He had been busy breaking in and training horses for most of the day, and was now relaxing with a book. Caleb had told him that he could have the next two days free from work, and he was looking forward to doing some riding that would take him miles away from the ranch. He enjoyed riding alone and exploring new territory.

For over a week he had spent time reading alone in the library. Leroy had not spoken to him since the wrestling contest, and had avoided him as much as possible, and as Lonzo thought about Leroy Parker, he smiled. The friendly and fearless Leroy had managed to impress Lonzo in a way that no one had done for a long time, and Lonzo had also detected in Leroy a kindred spirit. They were as different as two men could possibly be, Lonzo thought to himself, and yet they were very similar.

Lonzo smiled again as he thought about the other

thing he had recently noticed about Leroy Parker. Leroy had a sensitive side. Lonzo had been made aware of this because of the way that Leroy had avoided him and refused to speak to him after he had snapped so viciously at the young man following the wrestling contest.

Lonzo was still thinking about Leroy when he heard the movement of the latch to the outside door of the library, and then the door opened. A brief smile flickered in Lonzo's eyes when Leroy entered the room.

Leroy stood back by the door, looking slightly uncomfortable. He cleared his throat, and said in an unusually curt voice, 'I want to ask you something. . . .'

Lonzo grinned, 'So,' he said, 'I take it this means that you are talking to me now, and that you've stopped avoiding me and sulking.'

Leroy said with slight irritation, 'I admit that I have been avoiding you and not speaking to you, but I don't sulk!'

Lonzo's grin broadened, 'So what do you want to ask me?'

Leroy suddenly felt that this was a big mistake. Emmett had offered to be the one to ask Lonzo for his help in assisting Maria with her dancing, but Leroy had said that he would do it – he had to speak to Lonzo again sometime, but right now, he was wishing that he had let Emmett do the asking.

Seeing Leroy's hesitation, Lonzo said, 'I promise I won't bite!'

Leroy took a deep breath, and said that he was not asking for himself, but for Annie's friend, Maria Powell.

Lonzo was no longer grinning as he said, 'Go on. . . .'

'The thing is . . .' Leroy began in as cheerful a tone as

he could, 'Maria wants to be able to dance reasonably well at the dance being held at the eating house in four days' time, and she needs some help with her dancing. . . .' he paused, and Lonzo stared at him blankly.

Undaunted by Lonzo's apparent lack of interest, Leroy continued speaking, and trying to keep his voice cheerful, explained that he, Emmett and Annie wanted to help Maria learn to do the dance steps in time to the music, and that they were hoping that Lonzo would be willing to play the dance music for them on his fiddle.

When Leroy had finished speaking, Lonzo just stared impassively at him. Lonzo did not have much sensitivity in his nature, and Maria's problem with dancing did not seem that important to him – but he did feel a kind of liking for the spirited Maria, and he also realized that Leroy had pushed aside a lot of hurt and angry feelings to ask for his help, and he respected that.

Rather hesitantly, Leroy said as Lonzo stared at him, 'Maybe you could meet us on the northern range tomorrow morning. . . !'

Lonzo just carried on looking at Leroy, and gave no reply. He wasn't going to refuse to help Leroy and Maria, but he enjoyed teasing Leroy.

When Lonzo did not say anything, Leroy could feel his annoyance starting to surface, and he turned to leave.

'Hey, Parker,' Lonzo called him back, 'You haven't heard my answer yet!'

Leroy swung round to face him, and said fiercely, 'My name is *Leroy*, you might try using it sometime!'

Leroy very rarely lost his temper, but he felt suddenly infuriated by Lonzo's indifferent attitude, and the fact that

Lonzo seemed so determined not to become his friend.

Lonzo grinned somewhat mockingly; 'OK,' he said, 'Leroy,' and he emphasized the name, 'You haven't heard my answer yet!'

Leroy tried to control the fury that was welling up inside him, but his voice was full of raw emotion as he said, 'Why do you always insist on treating me like some kind of a fool?' and turned his head away.

Lonzo's mocking grin disappeared. He had never meant to evoke such anger and emotion in Leroy, and he felt almost sorry.

Lonzo said quietly, 'I can assure you, Leroy Parker, that treating you like some kind of a fool has never been my intention.'

Leroy took a few deep breaths to calm himself down, then turned back to stare curiously at Lonzo. He could sense that Lonzo had meant what he said, and he was surprised that Lonzo had let his unfeeling mask slip.

Lonzo very quickly realized that he had let his hard, impassive demeanour weaken for a second, and he felt embarrassed that he had allowed this to happen; trying to cover up his discomfort, he said harshly, 'What's in it for me?'

'What?' Leroy murmured.

'If I do play the fiddle for you,' Lonzo's voice was still harsh, 'What's in it for me?'

Slowly Leroy began to smile; he was starting to feel more like his usual amiable self, and suggested: 'You'd be helping Maria. . . .'

'I don't see anything in that for me,' Lonzo stated coldly.

'Well,' Leroy said genially, 'Maria is a friend of Annie and Annie's family, and you've played the fiddle for Annie and her family in their eating house a few times, so if you help Maria, you'll be helping Annie and her family, in a way. . . .'

Lonzo snorted, 'I got paid for playing the fiddle in the eating house. I didn't do it to help Annie and her family!'

'*Oh*!' Leroy said with a knowing grin. He would have to try a different incentive: 'In that case, how about I buy *all* your drinks at the dance that Jeremiah and Dinah are holding in four days' time?'

Lonzo appeared to think it over. Leroy watched him, hoping that Lonzo would allow him another glimpse of the real man beneath the uncaring façade.

Lonzo suddenly smiled. It wasn't his usual smug kind of a smile: it was a smile that lit up his whole face, and made him look so much younger. 'It's a deal!' he stated.

Leroy was pleasantly surprised to see the way Lonzo's features had softened with the huge smile on his face.

'You should do that more often,' he remarked.

'What?' Lonzo was puzzled.

'Smile like that, it makes you look almost human!'

After that, Leroy turned and left the library – but he was smiling as he went, and he felt an odd, warm glow inside him. He had seen a glimpse of the real Lonzo beneath the unfeeling mask, and he knew that he had been right in thinking that Lonzo was not as aloof and uncaring as he liked to make out he was.

Inside the library room, Lonzo was also smiling. Leroy Parker had somehow made a small dent in his hard-hearted armour, and for the first time in a long time, he felt as if he had met someone he could trust.

CHAPTER 6

The following morning, Leroy and Emmett awoke with the early light of dawn, but the bunk bed opposite to their own beds where Lonzo slept was unoccupied: clearly Lonzo was already up and about, and they hadn't heard him get up and leave the bunkhouse. Marvin Kilbey was still slumbering noiselessly in his bed.

Emmett was impatient for them to get started on their ride to the northern range – he was eager to see Annie again – but Leroy insisted on making them some breakfast in the cook shack. He fried some bacon slices in a pan on the hotplate of the wood-burning stove, and they sat down at the table to eat.

Leroy had told Emmett about the deal he had made with Lonzo the previous night in the library; Emmett, wondering about the deal, looked across at Lonzo's empty bed and said, 'I guess Lonzo must have woken up and galloped off somewhere before it was even light.'

'Yeah,' Leroy nodded, 'But he knows where to meet us.'

Emmett grinned, amused at Leroy's confidence in Lonzo. 'So you think he meant it when he made that deal with you last night about helping Maria. . . .'

'He meant it all right,' Leroy said with a smile.

It was still quite early in the morning, but the sun was already warm and bright as Leroy and Emmett rode out to the northern range of the Baxter ranch land. The two men didn't find Lonzo waiting for them near to Creek Hill, nor was there was any sign of Annie and Maria, but they did find that a few head of cattle had strayed away from the main herd and were grazing too close to a chain of hills on the edge of the range, and were therefore at risk from predators. They spent over an hour herding the straying cattle away from the hills and back to the safer Baxter grazing land. They spent another two or three hours checking over the range land for other strays, and herding them back, away from the hills.

It was getting towards the middle of the day, and with still no sign of Lonzo, Annie and Maria, the two men sat down in the rocks at the base of Creek Hill to eat some of their food provisions. They nibbled on strips of dried meat and listened to the sound of the nearby creek for a few minutes, all the while wondering why Lonzo, Annie and Maria were late in joining them. Emmett was physically aching to see Annie again, and he stood up and began to pace up and down beside the creek.

He abruptly stopped his pacing as both he and Leroy heard a sudden rush of hoofbeats and spotted two approaching riders. The two friends smiled when they saw that the riders were Annie and Maria, and Emmett gave a yell of joy. The girls had brought a picnic basket with them, and they all four sat down on the rocks near to the creek to enjoy the contents of the basket: tasty home-made meat and vegetable pies, and apple pies, and fruit cordial to drink.

Leroy said, 'We should leave some food for Lonzo,' still having faith that Lonzo would put in an appearance.

They sat contentedly eating and drinking for a while, then Leroy suggested to Maria that they try some dancing.

'Lonzo isn't here yet . . .' Maria began. She wasn't sure that she even wanted to try dancing again. She had only agreed to go with Annie to meet up with Leroy, Emmett and Lonzo, and had said she would try doing some dance steps because she didn't want to let her friend down.

'He will be. . . .' Leroy assured her.

Leroy pulled a protesting Maria to her feet, and on to the smooth patch of ground in front of them, and then he took her in a dance hold, and began to lead her into a waltz and talk her through the steps. He was patient and confident in his tuition, but Maria still tended to walk heavily through the steps with no sense of timing.

After about ten minutes of trying to dance with Maria, Leroy sighed to himself as he exchanged glances with Emmett and Annie. There was still no sign of Lonzo, and they couldn't wait for much longer. Leroy knew that he would now have to play the harmonica while Emmett and Annie helped Maria with the dance steps.

Lonzo had woken before dawn. He had dressed quickly in the half-light and eaten some sourdough biscuits for breakfast. He had taken some of the biscuits with him when he left the bunkhouse, without anyone hearing him, and had gone for a ride that had taken him out of the valley and to the entrance of Red Creek Canyon. Usually when he had two days of free time to himself he would camp out for the night in the Badlands, but he had given his word to Leroy that he would play the fiddle for Maria, and it was important to him not to let Leroy down.

Lonzo climbed down from his horse to wander round the entrance to the canyon for a while, and to give his horse time to rest; then he climbed back up into the saddle, and started the ride back to Caleb Baxter's ranch. He heard the sound of the harmonica while riding through the long grass on the northern range of the Baxter ranch land. He rode past a small bunch of foraging cattle, and then a few yards up ahead of him, near to the rocks at the base of Creek Hill, he saw the four of them: Leroy, Emmett, Annie and Maria.

Leroy was seated on one of the rocks playing the harmonica, while Emmett was dancing with Maria. Annie was sitting on a large boulder near to the creek watching them. Lonzo grinned as he guessed that the tune that Leroy was meant to be playing was 'Oh Susanna', but the notes were not quite right.

Annie was the first one to see Lonzo cantering up to them, and she jumped to her feet and called out a greeting to him.

Emmett and Maria stopped dancing, and Leroy ceased playing his not very melodious tune, and got up off the rock. Lonzo rode up closer to them and dismounted.

Lonzo tethered his horse to a nearby bush and smiled politely at Annie and Maria, who were both giving him rather approving looks. They had known him for about six months, which was when he had first arrived at Caleb's ranch, and they had immediately liked his good-looks and self-assured manner, and he was always courteous to them whenever he met them. Leroy and Emmett saw the favourable looks that the girls were giving to Lonzo, and Annie's face changed as she felt Emmett staring at her.

Lonzo nodded to Emmett before turning his attention to Leroy. He walked closer to him, and said casually, 'Morning, Leroy,' emphasizing the name as he smiled mockingly.

Leroy felt irritation start to rise in him at Lonzo's mocking attitude. The man was late, and he had to know that it was now past midday – but he managed to control his annoyance, and said mildly, 'You're late, it's past midday now.'

'Oh, is it?' Lonzo said with fake surprise. His mocking smile changed to more of a grin as he asked, 'Am I right in thinking that it was "Oh Susanna" that you were playing on the harmonica?'

Leroy refused to let Lonzo rile him further, and said with a grin, 'Hadn't you better get started on playing your fiddle?'

Amusement glimmered for an instant in Lonzo's eyes, then he went across to where his horse was tethered. He took a small fiddle and a bow out of his saddle-bags; the fiddle had been made out of a cigar box. He sat down unhurriedly on a rock near to where Leroy stood, and held the fiddle against his chest instead of under his chin. He drew the horsehair bow across the strings, and while Leroy and the others watched him, started to play.

69

They heard a horrid, screeching sound, and Lonzo gave a low chuckle at the stunned looks on the faces of Leroy and the other three. Then he drew the bow across the strings again, and started to play a waltz tune. He played with a supple and light bowing stroke and the notes were perfect. He chuckled again, as though amused by the fact that he had surprised them all.

Emmett, Annie and Maria started to laugh with some relief as they realized that Lonzo had only been trying to fool them.

'*By jingo!*' Leroy burst out with a huge smile on his face, 'You got a sense of humour, what other secrets are you hiding?'

Lonzo's eyes turned grave for a second. He was hiding a huge secret: no one at the ranch knew that he was the Sundance Kid, and he wanted to keep it that way. Emmett, Annie and Maria were still laughing, and only Leroy had noticed the way Lonzo's eyes had briefly changed; he wondered what else the enigmatic man was hiding.

Emmett took Annie in his arms and began to dance the waltz with her. They looked very happy together, and Leroy felt a sudden and fleeting sadness as he thought about Amy, the girl he had left behind. Then he sensed Lonzo's curious eyes on him, and knew that he had noticed his momentary sadness. He quickly put Amy out of his mind and turned to Maria, swiftly drawing her into his arms to dance the waltz.

Maria was anxious and awkward at first, but Leroy's casual manner soon put her at ease. She gradually began to relax as she danced. Lonzo played another waltz tune, then a polka and some square dancing tunes while the others danced to the music, and both Emmett and Annie, and even Lonzo, noticed how happy and confident Maria was beginning to look as she danced with Leroy. Her awkwardness seemed to have gone.

As Lonzo sat drawing his bow skilfully across the strings of the cigar-box fiddle and watching the others dancing, he felt like having some fun of his own. Leroy had been right, he did have a sense of humour, but it was a very mischievous, almost wicked one. He wanted to do something to annoy Leroy, but only in a friendly, prankish way – he didn't want to provoke the fierce anger in Leroy that he had aroused before.

Smiling mischievously to himself, Lonzo suddenly stopped playing, immediately compelling the others to stop dancing and look questioningly at him. Unconcerned by their questioning looks, Lonzo got up off the rock, and holding the fiddle in one hand, walked across to Leroy and Maria, and said to Leroy, 'I reckon it's my turn to dance with Maria now, I know some square dances that I can show her!'

But Leroy felt that he was making progress with Maria, and told Lonzo in a pleasant tone to stick to playing the fiddle. At which Lonzo grinned, and said, 'It's up to Maria whether she wants to dance with me!'

Leroy scowled, and he and Lonzo started to argue – though not aggressively – and while arguing, they began to step away from the others, and closer to the edge of the low bank of the creek. Emmett, Annie and Maria watched them in surprise at first, but then their surprise turned to laughter, as they were behaving just like two little boys quarrelling over a toy.

As he argued with Lonzo, Leroy suddenly became aware of the laughter coming from the three onlookers, and realized, with some disgust at himself, how pointless the argument with Lonzo was – and with that realization came the knowledge that Lonzo had yet again managed to irritate him.

Leroy felt angry at himself and Lonzo, and abruptly ended the argument by telling Lonzo to do as he liked. He turned away from him intending to stride away, but he turned so abruptly that his feet slipped on the edge of the bank, and he started to fall over backwards into the creek.

Lonzo made a grab for him, but he was still holding the fiddle and bow in one hand, and he missed. Leroy fell into the creek with a yell and a huge splash, landing with a jolt on his back. The creek was not too deep, but he still got soaked, and some of the sharp rocks scattered along the bed of the creek grazed his back.

He pulled himself up into a sitting position and looked up at Lonzo. There was a hint of laughter in Lonzo's eyes as he stood at the edge of the creek looking down on Leroy.

'Are you hurt?' Lonzo had the decency to ask, but his tone held no real concern, and the laughter was still in his eyes. Leroy somehow stopped himself from giving an unpleasant reply.

Lonzo grinned. He was about to jump into the creek to help Leroy out of the water, but Emmett, Annie and Maria had hurried over to join them, and it was Emmett who waded in to help Leroy to his feet and out of the creek. Leroy's clothes were soaked, and his body felt bruised and sore in places. Annie and Maria were sympathetic, but Leroy was sure that he could still see a hint of mirth in Lonzo's eyes.

Emmett started to dab at Leroy's wet clothes with his bandanna, and as he did so, Leroy said to Lonzo in irritation, 'You are the biggest pain in the ass I have ever met!'

He sounded really annoyed, but Emmett, who was standing next to him and still dabbing at his clothes, noticed that his partner was trying to hide a smile. Emmett shot a quick look at Lonzo, expecting him to give a harsh reply to Leroy, but he was surprised to see that Lonzo was looking at Leroy with what appeared to be a friendly glint in his usually cold eyes.

The glint of friendliness in Lonzo's eyes disappeared almost straightaway, but Emmett felt certain that he had seen it, and he realized in that instant that not only did Leroy feel a strange kind of kinship with Lonzo, but that Lonzo also felt a liking for Leroy.

Lonzo saw the surprise on Emmett's face, and he knew that for maybe half a second he had let some emotion show in his eyes. He felt embarrassed, and he wanted to get away quickly. He turned abruptly from the creek, pushed his way past Annie and Maria, and strode hurriedly over to the bush where his horse was tethered. But Maria ran up to him before he could get on it, and gave him the remainder of the pies, wrapped in tissue paper, from out of the picnic basket, and told him that Leroy had insisted on saving some of the food for him.

Lonzo gave her a brief smile as he took the food from her, and placed it, together with his fiddle and bow, in his saddle-bags. Then he jumped on his horse, and without a glance at any of the others, rode away.

Leroy watched him ride away with a sigh and a shake of his head.

CHAPTER 7

Three days later, in the early evening, the dance to celebrate Dinah's birthday was held in the eating house of Jeremiah and Dinah Baxter. The festivities were in the long dining room, and there was already a merry atmosphere, with the people of the valley enjoying the dancing and the food and drinks. A bulbous-shaped wood-burning stove stood at one corner of the room, and four large glass oil lamps spaced a few feet apart were hanging from ropes attached to wooden beams along the centre of the ceiling.

The room had been arranged to allow space in the centre for dancing, with tables and chairs spread out along one side. Sitting at some of the tables were groups of homesteaders and ranchers from all over the valley.

On the opposite side of the room, to the right of the entrance door, were three long tables. Two of the tables were laden with tasty home-made food. On the third table was a pail of beer and beer glasses, and two large punch-bowls with serving spoons and glasses. One of the punch-bowls was non-alcoholic. There was also whiskey to drink, but that would have to be paid for. Serving the whiskey, and keeping an eye on the food and drink, was Warren Baxter, the youngest son of Jeremiah and Dinah.

The musicians were two men playing fiddles, and two other men playing banjos, and they were standing at the far end of the room. Some of the ranch hands and home-steaders were already slightly drunk; their voices, accompanied by raucous laugher, were loud above the music. A slow waltz was being played, and several couples were dancing together in the middle of the room. Among the dancers were Jeremiah and Dinah Baxter (who were hosting the dance), and Caleb Baxter and his wife Elizabeth, a slim, blonde-haired lady. Jeremiah was tall and sinewy like his younger brother, Caleb. His wife, Dinah, looked a lot like their daughter, Annie, with the same curly brown hair.

Leroy and Emmett entered through the doorway just as the waltz music finished, and Emmett immediately spotted Annie and Maria. The young ladies were walking towards the food and drink tables, and they were both looking very attractive. Annie was wearing a long lilac dress, and her long, curly brown hair was piled up neatly on top of her head. Maria's long black hair was tied back with a ribbon, and she wore a long lemon and white dress. Emmett hurried over to intercept them, while Leroy lingered by the doorway.

The music started up again. Emmett took hold of Annie's hand, and after asking Maria to excuse them, he led her on to the dance floor. Maria walked on over to the food and drink tables; she glanced briefly at the two tables filled with the food, and then moved on to the third table, which was the drinks table, and where Warren was serving the whiskey. She was looking with interest at the alcoholic punch-bowl when Leroy went over to her. He was just going to ask her to dance with him when his attention was turned to someone else.

Leroy had not seen Lonzo enter the eating house – he didn't even know he was there until he suddenly appeared at the drinks table a few feet away from where Leroy was standing with Maria, and asked Warren to pour him a whiskey.

While Warren poured the whiskey, Lonzo turned his head to look at Leroy and Maria. He said with a mocking grin to Leroy, 'Evening, Leroy' – he emphasized the name – 'You fallen into any creeks lately?'

They had been working on different ranges, and had not seen much of each other since Leroy had fallen in the creek. Leroy gave Lonzo an annoyed look. Lonzo grinned again, then he smiled at Maria before taking some coins from out of a pocket in his pants to pay for the whiskey. Leroy reluctantly moved away from Maria and walked over to him. He said, 'We have a deal, remember? I'm paying.'

'Oh, yeah,' Lonzo said, and his eyes sparkled mischievously as he looked at Leroy, 'I forgot. . . .'

Leroy grunted, 'I doubt that. . . .'

The sparkle was still in Lonzo's eyes as he shrugged, and said, 'Well, maybe you can buy just this one drink for me, then we'll forget about the deal. . . .'

Leroy stared at him, puzzled by his words.

Lonzo gave a short laugh, 'Despite what you might think, I ain't *completely* heartless – and just in case you think I'm treating you like some kind of a fool – let's call it a kind of favour, a favour from me to you. . . .'

Lonzo then left Leroy to pay for the whiskey, and walked over to Maria, who was still standing by the punchbowl. He asked her to dance with him. She nodded, and walked quite confidently on to the dance floor ahead of him. Leroy and Lonzo both noticed the confident poise with which Maria walked. She no longer seemed to be worried about looking like a clumsy fool on the dance floor. Lonzo stopped to give a slight wink to Leroy before following her.

Leroy felt a little irked. He had wanted to dance with Maria, and Lonzo's wink told him that Lonzo must have guessed what was in his mind.

The musicians were playing a polka. Maria was a little awkward on her feet at first, but Lonzo said to her, 'Just listen to the music and remember the steps that Leroy showed you a couple of days ago, and you'll be fine.'

Maria smiled, and feeling encouraged by Lonzo, she soon overcame her clumsiness, and danced with faultless timing to the music.

Leroy stood by the drinks table, watching Lonzo and Maria dancing, and he felt his slight displeasure disappearing. Lonzo was a good dancer, and Maria, he was glad to see, looked like a natural dancer. It was almost impossible to believe that she had been worried about people laughing at her. Maria's parents and other family members were sitting with a group of homesteaders, and they were surprised, along with a lot of other people in the room, to see how elegant and confident she was in her dancing.

Warren's voice broke into Leroy's thoughts: he was asking about Lonzo's glass of whiskey. Leroy sighed – it didn't look as if Lonzo was in any hurry to come back and drink it.

'Keep it,' he said to Warren, 'until Lonzo comes back for it.' Then he went over to the pail of beer, dipped a ladle into it and filled a glass. Carefully avoiding the dancers, he made his way over to the other side of the room and sat down at one of the tables. But several of the rowdy ranchers and homesteaders sitting at the tables further up from him called out a greeting, and he went over and chatted to some of them. He was liked by almost everyone in the valley because of his friendly, helpful nature.

The night wore on, and more ranch hands entered the eating house, including Deke Hogan and Marvin Kilbey. These two went straight over to the table with the pail of beer on it, dipped two glasses into the pail and filled them, then crossed the floor to the tables to sit down. Hogan scowled at Leroy as he walked past him, but Kilbey chose to sit down at Leroy's table.

The next half hour passed by fairly uneventfully. Emmett and Annie stayed on the dance floor, and so did Lonzo and Maria, but when the slow waltz they had been dancing finished, Lonzo asked Maria if she would excuse him. Although he was enjoying dancing with her, he did not want Leroy to think that he was mocking him in some way by leaving the glass of whiskey that he had bought for him untouched on the drinks table with Warren for too much longer.

Maria felt disappointed – she had been enjoying dancing with her new-found confidence – but she nodded. They were standing near to some of the tables where the homesteaders and ranchers were sitting, so Lonzo walked away from Maria, expecting her to maybe join her family members at their table, and he headed for the drinks table. However, Maria did not get the chance to join her family at their table, because both Leroy and Marvin Kilbey had spotted her standing by the tables, and both men quickly sprang up out of their chairs with the intention of asking her to dance – but it was Kilbey who reached her first, and he was the one she agreed to dance with.

Leroy groaned to himself as he sat back down at the table again. It didn't look as though he was going to get a chance to dance with Maria.

Warren saw Lonzo approaching the drinks table, and handed him the glass of whiskey. Lonzo took the whiskey, and keeping out of the way of the dancers, strolled over to the tables on the opposite side of the room to find somewhere to sit. Leroy smiled at him in a friendly way as he approached the table where he was sitting.

Lonzo grinned and said, 'Thanks for the whiskey,' and then he sauntered past Leroy to sit down at an unoccupied table to the left of Leroy, between Leroy and Deke Hogan.

'Hey!' Leroy called to him, 'I promise I won't bite!'

Lonzo turned to look at him, and said with another grin, 'You surely can't want me to sit with you, I'm the biggest pain in the ass you've ever met!'

Leroy laughed, and said, 'I reckon I can overlook that!' and motioned Lonzo over with his hand.

Lonzo hesitated – he usually preferred to sit on his own – but as Leroy smiled and again motioned him over, he began to get to his feet. He had half risen out of his chair when there was a rush of movement and a lot of noise at the entrance door to the eating house. Barging their way through the door came a group of six ranch hands from the Cottonwood Ranch, the neighbouring ranch to Caleb Baxter, and following behind the ranch hands was the Cottonwood owner, Bart Jarvis. A few minutes earlier the Cottonwood men had all been drinking in the saloon, which stood to one side of the eating house, but they had been listening to the noise of the dance and wanted to join in.

The merry atmosphere in the room instantly changed. The musicians stopped playing, and low, concerned muttering could be heard coming from some of the folks in the room. Jeremiah Baxter and his brother, Caleb, were still on the dance floor with their wives, and they immediately stopped dancing at the sudden intrusion of the Cottonwood men, as did all the other dancers.

Jarvis and his ranch hands were not liked or trusted by anyone in the valley. They had long been suspected of rustling cattle from other ranchers at Browns Hole, and they had even tried to drive out a few homesteaders to take over their land. Jeremiah and his wife and family usually tried to put aside their concerns regarding the Cottonwood men. They would let them drink at the saloon, shop at the general store and eat at the eating house. It was easier that way, and it stopped any serious trouble from developing – but they didn't want the men to cause a ruckus at the dance. At Browns Hole, the usual tradition was, that all celebrations and dances were attended by most of the valley residents – but no one wanted Bart Jarvis or anyone who worked for him at their celebrations.

Lonzo did not go over to join Leroy. He stayed where he was and sat back down in his chair. Both he and Leroy felt uneasy when they saw that Archie Burdett, Seth Roebuck, Eli Slater and Bill Gooch, the four men who had caused trouble for Leroy and Emmett in Green River, were among the group of Cottonwood ranch hands.

Warren hurried over to the men as they barged their way through the door, and told them (not too impolitely) that they were not welcome at the dance, and that they would have to leave. Caleb and Jeremiah quickly ushered their wives off the dance floor and over to the side of the room where the ranchers and homesteaders were sitting. They were followed by all the other people who had been dancing, including Emmett and Annie, and Marvin Kilbey and Maria. They all stood in straggly groups muttering amongst themselves further up the room from the tables where Leroy, Lonzo, Hogan and the other valley residents were sitting.

The Baxter brothers then left their wives, and started to hurry across the room towards Warren. They knew that he would need help in dealing with Jarvis and his men. Three of Caleb's ranch hands followed behind them, but before they could reach Warren, Archie Burdett, who was at the front of the Cottonwood interlopers, laughed in Warren's face, and then thrust the young man aside with so much force that he went crashing down to the floor, striking his head on the corner of one of the food tables as he fell. He lay unmoving on the wooden floor.

Dinah screamed at seeing her son fall, and both she and Annie tried to run to him, but they were held back by Emmett and Caleb's wife, Elizabeth.

The room went very quiet and tense after Dinah's scream.

Caleb, Jeremiah and the three ranch hands were still hurrying anxiously towards the fallen Warren, but they were brought to a sudden halt as Archie Burdett and the five other Cottonwood ranch hands intercepted them with their guns drawn. Holding their guns on the Baxter men, the six Cottonwood men spread themselves out in a line in front of them, and in a brusque, commanding voice, Burdett ordered the five men to get their hands up.

The tension in the dining room could now almost be felt.

From where he sat at the side of the room, Leroy wanted to do something to help Caleb, but he knew that all he could do for the moment was just sit still. Emmett and Marvin Kilbey, standing in a group of people further up from Leroy, also felt like running forwards to help Caleb, and Maria urged them to, but they wisely stayed with the group.

Lonzo sat calmly drinking his whiskey, but he was watching the situation with Caleb and the Cottonwood men intently. He would give his help if he had to, but only when he felt that the time was right.

Bart Jarvis, the owner of the Cottonwood ranch, a scrawny-looking man with long grey hair, stood to one side of the doorway. He had a slight grin on his face as he watched Burdett and his other men.

Caleb, his brother Jeremiah, and the three ranch hands who were facing the guns of the six Cottonwood men, all stared at each other in dismay – they knew that trying to make a grab for their own weapons would only get them

83

all killed, so they grudgingly obeyed Burdett and raised their hands high. Burdett grinned at Caleb, and said, 'Let's hear you accuse me of rustling your stock now, Baxter!'

Caleb's face was red with fury as he glowered at Burdett. He had been in quite a few clashes with the man in the past regarding the rustling of his cattle, and he hated being forced to back down to the Cottonwood foreman. He felt like making a bodily charge at Burdett, but he knew that such a move would be foolish.

Burdett laughed scornfully, and then turned to look at Jeremiah, who was standing next to his brother, and said harshly, 'We don't take kindly to folks telling us that we are not welcome, Baxter, so if you want to avoid any one getting killed here, you'd better ask us to stay at this party!'

Jeremiah exchanged looks with Caleb: he was feeling as furious as his brother. He did not like being threatened in his own eating house and at his wife's party, but he knew that he would have to try to avoid any bloodshed. He was also worried about his son, Warren, whom he could see still laid out on the floor near the doorway. He looked towards Bart Jarvis, and shouted to him to call off his men.

Jarvis merely grinned derisively at him.

Leroy frowned as he observed Jarvis's derisive grin: the Cottonwood boss clearly approved of what his men were doing. Then four of Caleb's ranch hands, who were seated at a table to the right of where Leroy was sitting, looked meaningfully at each other, and keeping their movements slow, and their hands close to their guns, started to rise out of their chairs.

Leroy saw them starting to rise to their feet, and he

noted that their hands seemed to be very close to their guns. He clicked his fingers at them to get their attention, and when they looked his way, he motioned to them with his hand to sit down, and not to try anything: he knew that if the men did open fire on Jarvis and his men, then it might result in a lot of people getting killed.

The four men understood what Leroy was trying to say to them, and they also reconsidered what they were about to do, and realized that Leroy was right. It would be very dangerous for everyone in the room if they were to draw their guns and open fire, so they sat back down again.

Lonzo had seen Leroy signal to the four men, and he smiled approvingly. Not only did Leroy have a subtle toughness and a fearless nature, but he also appeared to have a wise head.

Jeremiah shouted again to Jarvis to call off his men. Jarvis grinned for a few more moments, then he said icily, 'I'll call my men off if you ask us all nicely to stay at your celebration.'

Jeremiah yelled back furiously to Jarvis, 'If you don't order your men to put their guns away and to get out of here right now, I'll ban all of you at the Cottonwood ranch from using my saloon, store and this eating house: I'm the owner and I can do that, and I'll hire help to keep you all out if I have to!'

His words caused an angry outburst of expletives from Burdett and the other Cottonwood ranch hands. Jeremiah's saloon, general store and eating house were the closest for miles.

Jarvis immediately lost his grin at the furious threat from Jeremiah. His eyes grew fierce, and he drew out his gun and moved away from the doorway to stand in line with Burdett and his other ranch hands. Seven guns were now trained on Caleb and Jeremiah Baxter, and Caleb's three men.

Jarvis's fierce eyes menacingly scrutinized the five men standing in front of him. He saw that sweat was beginning to glisten on the foreheads of the three ranch hands, and that all the Baxter men were fidgeting nervously.

Jarvis barked at them all to stand still, and then he walked up closer to the furious Jeremiah, looked him in the face and snarled out, 'You are in no position to make threats, Baxter – either you ask us to stay at your party, or we open fire and you die, and we'll also gun down anyone else who tries to intervene!'

He meant it. Everyone in the room knew he meant it. Jarvis and his men were ready and eager to shoot and kill the five men standing in front of them, and anyone else who tried to help them.

Jeremiah and Caleb exchanged looks again. They did not want to give in to the demands of Jarvis and his men, but they had the safety of everyone else in the room to consider, and Jeremiah desperately needed to check on his son.

'Well, Baxter!' Jarvis demanded, 'Are you going to ask us to stay?' and he aimed his gun at Jeremiah's chest.

The three Baxter ranch hands, who were standing next to Jeremiah, began to fidget nervously again; sweat was trickling in long streaks down their faces, and their eyes showed fear. They could no longer endure the mental anguish of their frightening situation, and they started to lower their hands in the hope of quickly drawing their guns before they were seen.

The tension in the dining-room was still very intense. Everyone was on tenterhooks watching the scene between the Cottonwood and the Baxter men, but only Leroy, Lonzo and Deke Hogan noticed that the three ranch hands were starting to lower their hands, and they felt alarmed: they knew that if they did manage to draw their guns and open fire, or if the Cottonwood men spotted them lowering their hands, then a ferocious gun battle would take place in the dining room and people would get killed or injured.

Hogan had felt out of favour with his boss, Caleb Baxter, lately, and he wanted to do something to impress him, and everyone else at Browns Hole. He was aware that at any second, the three ranch hands standing alongside Caleb and Jeremiah were going to draw their guns and open fire. He looked slowly around the room while trying to think of something to do (without getting hurt himself) to help and impress his boss.

His eyes were suddenly drawn upwards to the four large glass oil lamps hanging from ropes on the beams along the ceiling in the centre of the room. Two of the oil lamps were positioned above and between the group of Cottonwood men and the men from the Baxter ranch.

Deke Hogan grinned. He considered himself to be exceptionally fast and accurate with a gun, and he was certain that he would be able to draw out his gun and shoot down the two oil lamps that hung above and between the two groups of men facing each other before Jarvis and his ranch hands could notice what he was doing and open fire on him.

Hogan's right hand was hidden from view under the table, and he quickly pulled out his gun and aimed at one of the ropes holding the oil lamps. His intention was to split the rope from which the oil lamp hung with his first shot, and then to swiftly fire at the rope holding the other oil lamp, and bring both lamps crashing down between the Cottonwood men and the Baxter men, and thus causing a diversion.

Hogan's gun roared out twice, but it was not his bullets that brought the two oil lamps down with a tremendous shattering noise. Four shots were actually fired, but because of all the tense drama that was taking place in the room, no one was really sure of how many shots they had heard. Only one person saw what really happened.

The table that Lonzo was sitting at was a few feet behind and to the right of where Hogan sat, and he had witnessed the foreman pulling out his gun and aiming at the ropes holding the oil lamps. He had realized at once what Hogan was going to do, and had pulled out his own Colt Peacemaker gun in case Hogan failed to hit his targets.

Hogan's bullets missed the ropes, and Lonzo opened fire barely a split second after Hogan: in a whirlwind of motion, he fired at the ropes holding the oil lamps, severing the strands with his bullets. Then just as quickly, he placed his smoking Colt back inside his holster.

Only Leroy Parker had caught a glimpse of Lonzo's amazing speed and precision with a gun, and he smiled, feeling a surge of admiration for Lonzo – and he wondered how many more surprises Lonzo was hiding.

When the shots were first heard and the two oil lamps

began to plummet down from the beams, most of the people in the room had instinctively looked round, wondering who had fired the shots – and they saw Deke Hogan, sitting holding his gun and smiling as though in triumph. And Hogan himself assumed that his bullets had brought down the lamps.

Lonzo was happy for everyone to believe that Hogan was responsible for shooting down the lamps. He did not want anyone at Browns Hole to find out that he was also known as the Sundance Kid. He did not know that Leroy had witnessed his skill with a gun.

As the oil lamps suddenly and loudly crashed down in front of Bart Jarvis and his men, for an instant they were startled, and jumped back with cries of alarm. Shards of glass flew out at them, and some of the men even dropped their guns.

Standing opposite to them, the Baxter men had been equally startled by the loudly crashing lamps, and they too had to step back to try and avoid the shards of flying glass – but they got over their feelings of surprise and alarm more quickly than the Cottonwood men.

Jeremiah immediately ran over to his son, Warren, who had started to come round, but Caleb and his three ranch hands dodged the debris of the smouldering oil lamps and flung themselves at Jarvis and the other six hostile invaders. They started throwing punches at the men who were still disconcerted by the shock of the falling oil lamps.

Those Cottonwood men who had held on to their guns, tried to aim them at the oncoming attackers, but they were very soon disarmed. Emmett, Marvin Kilbey and some of the other ranchers and homesteaders ran over to join in the affray.

Flames were starting to rise up from the debris of the shattered oil lamps, but a major fire and catastrophe was averted by the quick thinking and actions of Lonzo and Leroy. The two men grabbed tablecloths from off some of the tables, and used them to smother the flames; they then joined the other men in fighting with the Cottonwood interlopers and throwing them out of the eating house.

In the early hours of the next morning when the sky was still dark, Leroy and Emmett, both with bruises on their faces from the brawl with the Cottonwood men, were sitting on the top rail of one of the corral fences at the Baxter ranch. The two friends had helped to clean up the dining room of the eating house, which had been left in a mess from the shattered oil lamps and the fight with Jarvis and his men, and they were feeling too restless for sleep. They talked about the events of the night before, and how lucky it was that no one had been killed in the tense and frightening incident that had taken place in the eating house.

Emmett then said, 'I ain't got no liking for Deke Hogan, but I reckon we should all be thanking him for shooting down those oil lamps and causing a distraction.'

Leroy sighed deeply. He knew the truth about what had really happened, but he felt reluctant to say anything. He had been thinking a few things over, and it was obvious to him that Lonzo did not want anyone to know about his skill with a gun as he had quite willingly let everyone believe that it was Hogan who had shot down the oil lamps.

Leroy also believed that he knew the reason why Lonzo wanted to keep his expertise with a gun a secret. Leroy had heard talk a few times in several different towns he had been in about a young man who was supposedly very fast and skilful with a gun. This young man was described as being extremely tough and surly, and he spoke with a slight eastern accent. He was known as the Sundance Kid. Leroy had caught a hint of an eastern dialect in Lonzo's voice, and he now believed that Lonzo was the very same.

Emmett heard Leroy's deep sigh, and he turned to stare at him in puzzlement. Leroy didn't want to betray Lonzo's secret, but Emmett was his partner, and he trusted him. He said quietly, looking at Emmett, 'It ain't Hogan we all should be thanking. . . .'

'What. . . ?' Emmett was bewildered.

Leroy's voice was louder as he said, 'Hogan's bullets missed the ropes . . .' he paused for a second, and then said, 'This *has* to be kept between us because I don't think he wants anyone to know, but it was Lonzo who shot down those oil lamps.'

'Lonzo!' Emmett gasped.

'Yeah,' Leroy nodded, and for a moment, admiration for Lonzo showed in his eyes, 'It seems our unfriendly and outspoken Lonzo is a wizard with a gun.'

Emmett asked in bewilderment, 'But . . . why is he willing to let Hogan have all the praise and thanks for what he did?'

Leroy gave a slight shrug, 'He must have his reasons.'

He did not tell Emmett that he believed Lonzo to be the Sundance Kid. That was one secret he *was* going to keep to himself.

Emmett asked, 'Does Lonzo know that you know?'

Leroy jumped off the rail of the corral fence before answering, 'No, he don't. And like I said to you before, this has to be kept between us.'

Emmett also jumped down off the rail, and the partners started to walk over to the bunkhouse to try and get some sleep – but before they reached the building, Emmett stopped walking, and asked, 'So just how good is Lonzo with a gun? You called him a wizard, and I know how good you are . . . .'

It was true. Leroy was a fast shooter and a good marksman.

Leroy smiled. Admiration showed again in his eyes, and he said, 'Lonzo's faster than me, I think he's faster than anyone I've seen so far, and even under pressure, he hits where he aims.'

Emmett gave a low whistle, and said, 'If he's faster than you, then he must be something special!'

'He is.' Leroy still smiled, and emphasized again that it had to be kept between the two of them.

Emmett grinned: it was quite obvious that Leroy felt a strong sense of loyalty towards Lonzo, and he got the feeling that sooner or later, Leroy would ask him about the possibility of them taking on another partner.

CHAPTER 8

It had been over three weeks since the traumatic incident at the dance, and following it, Jeremiah had allowed Bart Jarvis and his ranch hands to use the general store, but they were not permitted to enter the saloon or the eating house. Jarvis and his men were furious at this ban, and had made several attempts to barge their way into the buildings, but they had been forced out at gunpoint by Jeremiah and his sons, or by some of the men who worked for them.

Also since the incident at the dance, quite a few head of cattle had started disappearing from Caleb Baxter's eastern range land, and he strongly suspected that ranch hands from the Cottonwood ranch had been rustling his cattle. The eastern range of Caleb's ranch stretched for over six miles, and ended at the edge of an area of steep and rocky country that separated his land from land belonging to the Cottonwood Ranch. This area of broken country was difficult to cross, but there were a couple of narrow and level stretches of land virtually hidden in the rough terrain, and Caleb felt sure that Jarvis's men had been using these level strips of land to ride across to his range and rustle some of his stock.

Caleb wanted to thwart the rustlers somehow, or maybe even catch them, and he decided to send two of his men to one of his line shacks on the eastern range to keep an eye on the herds of cattle that were grazing there, and whose numbers had been slowly dwindling. He decided to ask Leroy and Emmett to ride out to the line shack on the eastern range. They would stay at the shack for about a month to watch over the cattle, after which time they would be replaced by two other ranch hands.

But two days before Leroy and Emmett were due to ride out to the shack, Caleb's brother, Jeremiah, rode up to the ranch house quite early in the morning to ask Caleb if one of his ranch hands could help him out in his general store for a while as two of his sons were away visiting friends. Jeremiah then rode back to his small community and left it up to Caleb to speak to his ranch hands and to ask one of them to go and help out at the store.

As it was early morning and not long past breakfast time, Caleb first stopped at the bunkhouses to see if any of his men were inside still eating breakfast. There was no one in the first bunkhouse, but in the second one he found Leroy, Emmett and Marvin Kilbey. Leroy and Emmett were sitting on their bunks and sorting through some things to take to the line shack, and Kilbey was sitting at the table in the cook shack, just finishing his breakfast before riding out to join Lonzo on the northern range.

Caleb walked through to the cook shack at the end of the bunkhouse, and said to Kilbey, 'Jeremiah needs someone to help in his store – how'd you like to go and work for him for a few weeks?'

Emmett and Leroy overheard him, and Emmett's face lit up – he was always eager to spend more time with Annie, and before Kilbey could say anything, Emmett shouted through to Caleb in the cook shack, 'I'd like to go and help at Jeremiah's store!'

Caleb smiled as he heard Emmett's eager shout – he knew how Emmett felt about Annie, and he stepped away from Kilbey and the cook shack, and walked up closer to Emmett, and stood looking at him with a knowing smile on his face. Leroy also had a huge smile on his face.

Their smiles caused Emmett to feel a little self-conscious at his excited outburst. He looked from Caleb to Leroy, and said rather uncomfortably, 'That is . . . if it's OK with you two?'

'You're supposed to be going to the line shack with Leroy,' Caleb reminded him. Emmett's face fell.

'It's OK,' Leroy said cheerily to Caleb, 'One of the others can go to the line shack with me – let Emmett go work at Jeremiah's store if he wants to!'

Caleb did not want to disappoint Emmett, so he agreed the decision with Leroy, then asked him how he felt about Lonzo accompanying him to the line shack. Caleb had a lot of respect and liking for Lonzo. The sandy-haired young man was a very willing and dependable worker, but Caleb was aware that the amiable Leroy Parker found the rather unfriendly Lonzo to be particularly annoying. Leroy's cheerfulness seemed to fade, and he hesitated, but Emmett smiled – he knew what his partner's answer would be.

Leroy gave a kind of resigned sigh, and said to Caleb, 'I guess I can put up with Lonzo's company for a few weeks.' Emmett chuckled to himself at Leroy's answer.

Caleb said, 'It's settled then,' and left the bunkhouse.

Emmett chuckled again. Leroy gave his partner a hard stare and asked what was so funny.

'Oh,' Emmett smiled innocently, 'It's just the thought of you having to *put up* with Lonzo's company for a few weeks. . . .'

'I ain't too pleased about it!' Leroy said indignantly.

Emmett laughed, 'You got a liking for Lonzo', he said, 'Why don't you just admit it?'

Marvin Kilbey could be heard laughing in the cook shack.

Leroy grunted, and started sorting through his things again, but keeping his gaze firmly away from the amused Emmett, he did admit something to himself: that next to Emmett, Lonzo was the only man he would like beside him if there was any trouble with the rustlers – and it wasn't because he believed Lonzo to be the Sundance Kid. It was because he knew that Lonzo was calm and fearless in a dangerous situation, and that he wasn't the type to run out on a companion – and, he finally admitted to himself, it was because he *liked* the man, and felt an increasing kinship with him.

A day later, and roughly an hour before midday, Leroy and Lonzo started out on their ride to the line shack.

The day was warm with plenty of sunshine, and the first two miles of the ride were through lush, natural meadowlands. A mile further on past the meadows they rode through an area of grassland that was interspersed in places by shrubs, trees and natural springs that seeped from the ground. At times while riding through the grassland they passed small herds of Baxter's cattle.

During the ride to the shack, Leroy chatted away almost non-stop. He talked for several minutes about Mike Cassidy, the man who had taught him and Emmett a lot about ranching and shooting – and while talking about Mike, he mentioned the short time that he and Emmett had spent rustling with Mike, though he quickly pointed out that he wouldn't rustle from anyone whom he considered to be a friend.

'I like to call myself Leroy Cassidy at times,' he stated with a cheery smile to Lonzo, 'in honour of Mike.'

Lonzo tried to shut his ears to most of Leroy's ceaseless chatter. The only response he made to it all was a sort of non-committal grunt. Leroy was by nature a talkative and sociable person, and he was finding it hard to get used to Lonzo's quietness. They were about two miles from the line shack when Leroy tried to get a verbal response from Lonzo by saying, 'I still don't know if Lonzo is your first or last name . . .'

'No, you don't . . .' Lonzo said impassively.

Leroy sighed wearily, and asked, 'Are you from the east? I once had a neighbour who came from the east, and the way you speak sometimes reminds me of him.'

Lonzo gave him a hard glower. Leroy groaned to himself as he realized that he had made a mistake in asking about the east. He had forgotten momentarily that Lonzo wanted to keep his identity of the Sundance Kid a secret.

97

Leroy said quickly, 'I ain't trying to pry into your past or anything like that, I'm just trying to have some sort of conversation with you – I just ain't the quiet type.'

Lonzo's hard glower slowly turned into a smile, and he muttered, 'I bet no one's noticed that!'

Leroy laughed, 'Well . . . at least you still got your sense of humour!'

The day felt a lot warmer when, some fifteen minutes later, Leroy and Lonzo rode out of the grassland and into an area of rough country. They followed along a wide, rocky and uneven trail that was lined by large boulders, spiky bushes and clumps of trees for a mile or more to the line shack. The shack stood on a level piece of ground near to the foot hills of Cold Spring Mountain. It was a one-roomed cabin built of logs, with a small porch attached to the outside. There was a small fenced corral to the side of the shack, so the two men saw to their horses, and then let them loose in it.

Carrying their saddle-bags and other gear, Leroy and Lonzo entered the shack and glanced around. There were two small windows, one on each side of the doorway. A pot-bellied stove with a flat top that could be used for cooking stood against one wall, and there were a couple of long shelves fixed to another, one stacked with tinned goods and storage jars, the other with metal plates, bowls and cups, along with cast-iron pans and skillets.

Two narrow wooden beds each with a mattress, blankets and pillows were wedged against the back wall. There were hooks on the walls to hang clothes on. A wooden table and two chairs stood in the centre of the room; a large oil lamp and coffee pot stood on top of the table.

Leroy went over to the shelves and studied the contents of the tins. There were beans, ham, fruit and vegetables, and also tins of condensed milk. Caleb liked to keep the line shacks well stocked with provisions. Leroy turned to Lonzo with a broad grin, and said, 'Well, I guess we won't starve while we're here!'

They opened a tin of ham and sat down at the table to eat, and Leroy chatted away merrily for most of the meal. Lonzo sighed wearily at times, indicating that he thought Leroy talked too much, then finally he said with a scowl, 'I bet Emmett's real glad to be away from your non-stop jawing.'

Leroy only laughed; he was finding it easier to control the irritation that Lonzo usually stirred in him. He said cheerily while looking across the table at Lonzo, 'Emmett's my partner, and he puts up with anything from me . . . it's what partners do, they work and ride together, and they put up with anything from each other. . . .'

Lonzo grunted without looking at him, and concentrated on eating.

Leroy laughed again, and Lonzo looked up at him – and then, for a split second before Lonzo swiftly turned his eyes away, Leroy was able to look straight into Lonzo's steel-like, grey-blue eyes, and he felt a strong, almost spiritual connection with him.

Leroy realized then that Lonzo felt the same kind of kinship with him that he felt whenever he was near Lonzo – and it made him want to know more about the reserved, sandy-haired young man.

'What about you?' Leroy asked Lonzo, 'Do you have a

friend or partner somewhere that you sometimes team up with? Or do you always ride and work alone?'

Another scowl appeared on Lonzo's face. Leroy assumed that he was going to get an angry reply, and he said, 'Sorry if I'm prying again.'

But the scowl on Lonzo's face gradually disappeared – and indeed the more time that he spent with Leroy Parker, the more he was finding it impossible to stay angry with him, and the more he was also aware of the kindred spirit that existed between the two of them.

Lonzo looked down at his food. He felt uneasy about the affinity he felt with Leroy, and when he spoke it was in a curt tone. He said, 'I had a couple of friends at one time, and they were kind'a like partners, but they double-crossed me, and that taught me that you can't trust anyone. So the last thing I want or need is a *partner.*'

Leroy did not say anything straightaway: he just stared intently at Lonzo as he looked down at the table. One of the many things that he had sensed about Lonzo was that he would make a true and loyal friend or partner to someone if given the chance, and that all he would ask for in return was the same kind of loyalty; in truth, a man after his own heart – and Leroy's next words came blurting out before he could stop them.

He said in a very earnest tone, 'You can trust me, I'd never double-cross you if you were my partner. . . .'

After he said this there was an uncomfortable atmosphere in the room. He had spoken like this on a sudden impulse, and he was now wishing that he hadn't. So OK, he knew that Lonzo felt the same kind of affinity that he did, but they hadn't known each other all that long, and they were far from being partners – in fact they weren't even friends, so why would Lonzo care if he could trust Leroy or not?

Lonzo slowly lifted his head to look at Leroy, with bewilderment flashing in his eyes. Leroy's words had completely confused him. Why would he say something like that? What point was he trying to make? In his own mind he was thinking they weren't partners, they weren't even *friends* – they were just two men who happened to be working at the same ranch together. The fact that they might feel a kind of kindred spirit was irrelevant.

The confusion that was whirling around in Lonzo's head caused him to react angrily, and he burst out with a cutting harshness to his voice, 'Well, that's good to know, but why would I care if you double-crossed me or not, you ain't my partner, you ain't even a friend!'

Leroy lowered his head: clearly Lonzo's cruel and biting words had hurt him deeply.

Lonzo regretted his angry outburst as soon as he saw how much his words had hurt Leroy. He had forgotten about the sensitive side of Leroy's nature – but he did not apologize.

After finishing their meal, Leroy and Lonzo left the shack and went over to the corral to catch and saddle their horses. There was an uneasy silence between them, and Leroy avoided looking at Lonzo.

They had already agreed beforehand that they would ride together through the half mile or more of rough country, and then they would split up to keep a watch on the several herds of cattle that were grazing in the grassland

and meadows. Leroy was riding ahead of Lonzo as they cantered along the rough trail that led away from the shack,
and he was still riding ahead as they rode into the grassland
and spotted a small herd of cattle to the right of them.

He reined his horse to a stop, and as Lonzo rode up to
him, just muttered something about staying in the grassland to watch the herd they could see to the right of them.
He expected Lonzo to carry on riding into the meadows
beyond to look for other groups of cattle – but he didn't,
he reined his horse in next to Leroy, and stared at him for
a long moment.

Leroy was conscious of this, but his feelings were still
bruised, and he wouldn't look at Lonzo, but just stared
straight ahead. Another minute passed by, and then Lonzo
said brusquely: 'I don't know which I find the most annoying, your endless jawing, or your sulking!'

Leroy felt almost compelled to laugh at those words: he
turned to look at Lonzo, and smiled. With his good
humour restored, he said with a touch of cheeriness, 'I
told you before, I don't sulk!'

'Yeah, you do!' Lonzo's voice was rough, but then he
took a deep breath. They might not be partners or friends,
but he did trust Leroy, which was a rare thing for him, and
he still regretted his harsh and angry words. He waited a
second, and said in a more reasonable tone, 'Maybe I
shouldn't have yelled at you, but I don't know what point
you were trying to make – it's like I said, we ain't partners,
you already got a partner . . . we ain't even friends, so why
would you say something like that?'

Leroy knew it was the closest thing to an apology that
he was going to get. With a carefree shrug and a smile, he

said, 'Forget it, I don't even know why I said it. . . .' He suddenly laughed, 'Anyway, a partnership between you and me ain't ever likely to happen, it would be a disaster, wouldn't it? I mean, with you and your plain speaking, and me and my "sulking" as you so nicely put it. . . .'

A faint suggestion of a smile appeared on Lonzo's face, and he was just about to pull on his horse's reins to ride away, when a thought struck him. He said to Leroy, 'It might be a good idea for us to have some sort of signal between us, in case one of us should meet up with the rustlers and get into trouble while on our own. . . .'

'What sort of signal?' Leroy queried.

'I was thinking of whistling a tune.'

'I don't know about that,' Leroy said a little doubtfully, 'Maybe firing two shots would be better?'

Lonzo grinned, and started to whistle a few notes from 'Oh Susannah'; then he switched to 'Sweet Betsy from Pike', adding a few odd notes in places.

Leroy laughed, 'I ain't so sure that'll work!'

Lonzo asked him to try and copy his whistle. Leroy attempted to whistle the tunes in exactly the same way that Lonzo had whistled them, and with the same odd notes included. He whistled them several times until Lonzo nodded his approval.

'I still ain't so sure it'll work,' Leroy remarked, 'What if we're miles away from each other? We wouldn't hear it!'

Lonzo shrugged, and pulled on his horse's reins to ride away into the meadows. 'Then you'll just have to fire the two shots.'

They met up at the shack in the evening, when they lit the

stove and cooked a meal. Lonzo yet again surprised Leroy with his cooking skills. After they had eaten, they took the two chairs outside on to the porch to sit in the cool of the evening.

Lonzo had brought his fiddle with him, and after some coaxing from Leroy, he played a few tunes. Leroy sometimes joined in the tunes on his harmonica, and Lonzo would just raise his eyebrows when Leroy played the wrong notes. Later, they took turns in watching the cattle throughout the night. One of them would do part of the night watch for up to two hours, and the other would take over for the next two hours.

Just after sunrise on the third day at the shack, Lonzo woke up and brewed some coffee. He had a gulp of the strong brew and glanced across the room at Leroy who was still asleep. Leroy had done the last watch of the night and had only been asleep for a couple of hours. Lonzo went over to him to wake him up to ride out and keep watch over the cattle, but then he had a change of heart, and decided to leave him to sleep. He took a small supply of biscuits and dried meat with him, and left the shack.

About thirty minutes or so after Lonzo had ridden away from the shack, four men were riding along one of the narrow and level strips of land that were almost hidden in the rugged terrain that separated the Cottonwood ranch land from the Baxter range. The width of the strip allowed for two men to ride alongside each other, with a few feet to spare on each side. The men were riding slowly and keeping a watchful look around them. They were on their way to seek out and rustle a small bunch of cattle from

Caleb Baxter, as they had been doing at various times during the past three weeks.

The four men were Archie Burdett, and his usual three companions, Eli Slater, Bill Gooch and Seth Roebuck.

The level strip of land came to an end just yards away from the line shack, and Burdett pulled his horse to a sharp stop when he spotted Leroy's horse in the corral next to the shack. When Burdett saw it, he guessed that a ranch hand of Baxter's was staying in the shack for the purpose of watching over the cattle.

Burdett's three cohorts hastily reined in when he did. Burdett said to them with annoyance in his voice, 'One of Baxter's ranch hands must be staying in the shack.'

Eli Slater rubbed his whiskery chin and said gruffly, 'Yeah, Baxter must be on to us.'

Seth Roebuck suggested sneaking up to the shack to take the man inside by surprise.

'No', Burdett said with a shake of his head, 'That's too risky, he might hear us. We'll stay out of sight somewhere nearby and catch him unawares when he leaves the shack.'

His three companions nodded in agreement, and the four men dismounted. They led their horses past the line shack and on to the rough trail that led into the grassland, and hid amongst a clump of cottonwood trees on the right of the trail.

Leroy woke up to the smell of coffee. There was no sign of Lonzo in the shack, and he guessed that he had left him to sleep.

Leroy quickly finished dressing. The coffee was still warm, and he poured some of the brew into a tin mug and took a long drink. He nibbled a few biscuits, and took a handful with him as he left the shack and headed for the corral and his horse. A few minutes later he was riding along the rough stony trail towards the grassland. He finished nibbling on a biscuit as he rode slowly towards a bunch of cottonwood trees up ahead of him on the right of the trail.

Obviously Leroy didn't know that Burdett and his cohorts were hiding and watching in the trees, but as he rode closer, and was roughly eight to ten feet away, he thought he heard a horse neighing from in amongst the trees. He pulled up his horse and stared at the trees. He couldn't see anything suspicious, but he felt very uneasy. He didn't want to risk making a move towards his gun, and he tried to remember the whistle signal between himself and Lonzo.

He started to whistle a few notes from 'Oh Susannah', then switched to 'Sweet Betsy from Pike', adding in the odd notes that Lonzo had taught him, and hoping that he had remembered the signal correctly. He had just started to whistle 'Oh Susanna' again when Archie Burdett and Seth Roebuck stepped out from the trees with their guns drawn.

Burdett had instructed Slater and Gooch to stay in the trees out of sight and to be ready to give help if needed, for although they had only seen one horse in the corral, they knew there was still a possibility that another of Caleb Baxter's ranch hands might be staying at the shack with Leroy, and that he might be riding somewhere nearby.

Leroy did not try to reach for his gun – he knew he would never make it – but it was not in his nature to panic. He sat still on his horse and gave a cheerful smile to

Burdett and Roebuck as they walked up to him and stood in front of his horse.

'Good morning,' Leroy said pleasantly to Burdett and Roebuck.

Burdett grinned: he was inwardly elated that it was Leroy who was staying in the shack, and that he had him at a disadvantage. He had not forgotten what had happened at the saloon in Green River, or the incidents in the past involving himself, Leroy and Caleb Baxter. He snarled out, 'It's not such a good morning for you, Parker: throw down your gun and don't try anything!'

Burdett intended to kill Leroy, but he was going to make him suffer first. Leroy's smile disappeared as he slowly took his gun from out of its holster and threw it to the ground.

Burdett carefully stepped around from the front of Leroy's horse to stand beside it. He kept his gun on Leroy all the time, then told him in a sharp tone to get down and to put his hands up. Leroy slowly climbed down from his horse. He stood in front of Burdett and his threatening gun, and raised his hands up high above his head.

Burdett stepped up closer to Leroy, and then without warning, rammed his left fist viciously into Leroy's stomach. Leroy doubled over, gasping for air and moaning in pain while holding his stomach. Burdett said callously, 'That's for all the grief you caused me in Green River!'

Roebuck moved round from where he had been standing at the front of Leroy's horse to stand beside Burdett. The two Cottonwood men grinned at Leroy's suffering. Leroy was still bent over, holding his throbbing stomach muscles and gasping for air.

'Stand up straight, Parker!' Burdett barked out, 'And put your hands back up high, unless you want another thump in the gut!'

Slowly and painfully Leroy straightened up and raised his hands back up above his head. He was still gasping a little, but he stared at Burdett with a steady, unafraid gaze.

'Is there just you staying at the shack?' Burdett rasped. He was anxious to know if there was another Baxter ranch hand staying at the shack with Leroy.

Despite the throbbing pain of his stomach, Leroy tried to smile as he asked, 'Is there just Roebuck here with you?' He knew that it was unusual to see Burdett with only Seth Roebuck, and that he was normally accompanied by Eli Slater and Bill Gooch as well.

Leroy was worried that Slater and Gooch might be staying hidden in the trees in case someone should suddenly appear on the scene to help him.

Burdett cursed at Leroy's question, and Leroy thought that he was about to be punched in the stomach again. Certainly it was in Burdett's mind to thump Leroy again, but then his eyes glinted with malice: he had thought of another way to cause suffering, and finally death, to Leroy.

Burdett told Roebuck to keep Leroy covered with his gun while he went back into the cover of the trees for his horse. Seconds later, he came back out of the trees with it, and led it over to where Roebuck and Leroy were standing. There was a coiled rope slung across the saddle horn, and after taking the rope off the pommel, Burdett grinned at Roebuck.

Seth Roebuck grinned back at him. He knew what Burdett had in mind. At a nod from Burdett, Roebuck moved to stand behind Leroy. He dug the muzzle of his gun into Leroy's back and told him to lower his hands and to put his palms together in front of him so that Burdett could tie his wrists.

Leroy could feel Roebuck's gun digging into his back, and he could do nothing but obey. He lowered his hands and placed his palms together in front of him. A smirk was on Burdett's face as he uncoiled the rope and used it to bind Leroy's wrists tightly together; then keeping hold of the other end of the rope, he mounted his horse and gave a short, powerful tug on the rope. Leroy was pulled off his feet by the force of the tug, and jerked face down on the hard ground.

Burdett laughed, 'This is where you pay for all the aggravation that you've caused me, Parker.'

Seth Roebuck also laughed, and hidden in the trees, Slater and Gooch moved into a position that gave them a better view of the trail and of what Burdett was doing to Leroy. They grinned at each other: just like Roebuck, they knew what Burdett had in mind.

Lying helpless in the dirt with his hands tied to the rope, Leroy felt a sudden, involuntary shiver as he realized what Burdett was about to do to him: he was going to drag him along the ground behind his horse until he was dead.

Burdett dug his spurs into the horse's flanks: it sprang forwards, but luckily for Leroy, not into a full gallop. Leroy was dragged and bumped along the rough, rocky trail, grazing his chin, arms and knees.

Burdett cantered past the cottonwood trees where Slater and Gooch were hiding, and he was laughing wildly. He deliberately kept to the edge of the trail so that he could drag Leroy through the thorny bushes and rocks lining the path. Most of Leroy's body was badly gashed by the jagged rocks and spiky bushes, and the pain he felt was sharp and intense.

Burdett only cantered for a few yards past the trees, then suddenly swung his horse around to ride back towards Roebuck, and as he rode up to Roebuck, he wheeled his horse round again to ride up past the trees, dragging Leroy in a kind of circular movement. He rode up past the trees again, then whirled round to canter back to where Roebuck stood.

Leroy's painful ordeal did not last for much longer. For a fourth time Burdett had spurred his horse into a fast canter past the trees where Slater and Gooch were hidden, when there was the sound of thundering hoofbeats. The ground seemed to shake, and in a whirlwind of movement and dust, a horse and rider galloped on to the scene.

At the very instant he appeared, and before any of the Cottonwood men had time to react, or even to realize that he was there, and while his horse was still in full gallop, Lonzo fired off two rapid shots. He did not shoot to kill – he didn't want to kill anyone unless he had no other choice – but one of his bullets severed the rope that Burdett was using to drag Leroy across the ground, and the other the reins that he was holding in his other hand.

Burdett's startled horse came to a sudden sliding stop, and Burdett was thrown forwards. The horse snorted and reared up, and Burdett was jerked backwards and out of the saddle. He hit the ground hard, striking his head on a rock, and lay motionless on his back. In the next second, Lonzo was galloping towards Seth Roebuck, who stood no more than a stone's throw away, staring at him in stunned amazement.

As Lonzo fast approached him, Roebuck shakily tried to aim his gun. Lonzo pulled his horse to a halt and aimed his gun at Roebuck, telling him to drop his weapon and to get down on his knees with his hands behind his head.

Roebuck did not need to be told twice, having just witnessed Lonzo's remarkably fast shooting. He looked fearful as he quickly threw his gun away across the ground and dropped down to his knees with his hands clasped behind his head – but he wondered anxiously why Slater and Gooch had not opened fire yet from the trees.

Eli Slater and Bill Gooch were still keeping out of sight in the clump of cottonwood trees on the edge of the trail. From their hiding place, they peered out at the motionless form of Archie Burdett lying on the trail just a few yards from them.

Lonzo's sudden and dramatic appearance, and the events directly following this, had all happened too quickly for them to do anything or even *think* of doing anything. Lonzo had burst upon the scene like a thunderbolt, and his quick-fire actions had temporarily shocked them into a sort of dazed stupefaction – but they were now beginning to recover from their bewilderment, and while keeping low in the undergrowth, they moved forwards a little more, and crouched down amongst a group of huge rocks and thick bushes at the front of the trees.

Now that he had dealt with Burdett and Roebuck, Lonzo's next thought was for Leroy. He climbed down from his horse, and shot an anxious glance across at Leroy while keeping his eyes and his gun on the two Cottonwood men.

Leroy was lying near to where Burdett lay. His face was to the ground, his wrists were still bound, and he wasn't moving. Lonzo started to hurry over to Leroy to check on him, but then stopped – he was standing in the best position to watch both Roebuck and Burdett, and he knew they were both devious men: Roebuck could be feigning his fear, and Burdett feigning unconsciousness. He decided to stay where he was for the moment, and called out Leroy's name, hoping that he hadn't passed out and wasn't too badly injured.

Fortunately, Leroy was conscious, and he heard Lonzo call out to him. He felt dazed as he slowly lifted his head to look at Lonzo. Several cuts were visible on his face, and most parts of his body seemed to be throbbing with pain. He lowered his head again and lay still for a second, then he groaned and coughed, and as his mind became clearer, he slowly and carefully hauled himself up into a sitting position. He started to examine himself gingerly to see how badly injured he was – fortunately he did not appear to have suffered any broken bones. He then began to try and loosen the rope around his bound wrists. Blood dripped from the grazes on his hands.

Lonzo watched him; he was thinking of going over to help him, but the rope binding Leroy's wrists had already been loosened from scraping along the ground, and he was soon able to free his wrists himself. He didn't try to stand up straightaway as he was feeling groggy and in considerable pain – but all his physical distress soon left his mind as he remembered Eli Slater and Bill Gooch, and his worry that the two men might be hiding in the clump of cottonwood trees on the right of the trail. And as he glanced anxiously at the rocks and bushes in front of the trees, he thought he heard a rustling sound.

Leroy yelled at Lonzo to get down, but his voice was weak and Lonzo didn't hear him. He lurched to his feet and yelled again at Lonzo to get down.

This time Lonzo heard him, and although he didn't know why Leroy was yelling at him to get down, he trusted him, and so dropped down into the brush on the opposite side of the trail to Leroy. And sure enough, as Lonzo hit the ground and Leroy, too, fell back down again, shots were fired from the direction of the trees. Seth Roebuck, who was still on his knees, quickly fell forwards on to his face when he heard the shots, though he kept his hands clasped behind his head.

Slater and Gooch were concentrating most of their fire at Lonzo. They were reluctant to fire too much at Leroy as he was lying quite near to Burdett and they were afraid of hitting their friend. They were also trying not to hit Roebuck, who was lying close to Lonzo.

The brush that Lonzo was lying in was sparse and offered little cover, and he couldn't move as Slater and Gooch continued to fire almost unceasingly at him. All he could do was try to keep as low as possible until he got a chance to use his gun.

Leroy knew that Lonzo was in a risky position, but he needed to get his hands on a gun to be able to help him. He glanced at the motionless form of Burdett, and began to scramble the short distance across the ground towards him. He kept low and close to the rocks at the side of the trail for some cover. Bullets whizzed all around him as he reached Burdett and grabbed his gun from its holster. He then took shelter behind a small boulder to the side of Burdett.

Sheltering behind the boulder, Leroy was only a few feet away from the bushes and rocks where Slater and Gooch were firing from. He couldn't actually see the two men, but he saw the smoke from their guns, which gave away their positions, and he caught a brief glimpse of sunlight glinting on metal as they continued to fire. He fired off two shots where he believed the men to be, hoping to draw their fire off Lonzo.

His shooting was fast and precise, and a shrill cry of pain rang out: the bullet had nicked Bill Gooch's ear lobe, and he could be heard cursing. It brought an admiring smile to Lonzo's face.

Gooch's injury caused a respite in the shooting from the rocks and bushes, and Leroy was quick to take advantage of the lull, and loosed off a shot again. Lonzo lifted himself up and fired with him, and another shriek was heard as a bullet seared across Slater's cheek bone.

Leroy and Lonzo fired again. Their shots were frighteningly close to Slater and Gooch, and the two men shouted out in surrender. Both their guns were thrown out from the rocks and bushes, and a second later, they stepped out themselves with their hands held high. Blood leaked from Gooch's ear injury, and was streaked across Slater's right cheek bone just below his eye.

Lonzo quickly reloaded his Colt Peacemaker gun and stood up. He kept the gun on Slater and Gooch, and shouted out to Seth Roebuck to get up and to walk over and stand beside his companions. Roebuck stood up, and keeping his hands behind his head, did as he was told. Burdett was still lying as though unconscious.

Leroy got rather unsteadily to his feet. His face was pale, and his shirt and pants were badly torn in several places, exposing blood-streaked cuts and gashes.

'Are you OK?' Lonzo called brusquely to him. Leroy mumbled that he was fine.

Lonzo could see that he was far from being fine, but he did not comment on the fact, but instead told Leroy to get some rope, and to tie up the three men while he kept his gun on them.

The rope that Burdett had used to drag Leroy along the ground behind his horse was lying a few feet away, and Leroy limped over to it. He assumed that he and Lonzo would be taking the four Cottonwood men back to the ranch for Caleb to deal with.

Lonzo tossed him a knife, and Leroy cut the rope into several long strips. The painful gashes on his hands made him wince a few times as he did so. He then tied the hands of Roebuck, Slater and Gooch behind their backs using the strips of rope, but he found it difficult to tie them securely because of the cuts on his hands.

Lonzo noticed this and strode over to him. He handed Leroy his gun, telling him to watch the men while he checked their bonds, and to keep an eye on the unconscious Burdett. In fact he tightened the ropes binding their wrists much more than was really necessary, causing them to gasp.

Leroy watched Lonzo with some curiosity. He knew there was no need to tighten the ropes so excessively, and then suddenly realized that somewhere deep inside Lonzo there was a ruthless streak.

The wounded Bill Gooch and Eli Slater started to protest about the ropes being too tight, but Lonzo ignored them. He went over to where Burdett was lying, turned him over on to his stomach and began tying his wrists. The Cottonwood foreman groaned and regained consciousness as Lonzo did so, and tried to put up a struggle as he became aware of what was happening, but Lonzo tied him securely, and again, unnecessarily tightly. He pulled Burdett to his feet, and dragged him over beside his three cohorts. Burdett was angry with them for not getting the better of Leroy and Lonzo, and glared at each of them in turn.

Lonzo took back his gun from Leroy and holstered it, at the same time giving Leroy a close look, silently checking that he was not about to pass out.

Burdett turned his angry glower on Leroy and Lonzo, and growled out, 'I guess you'll be taking us to Baxter now.'

Leroy nodded. Lonzo, however, gave Burdett a faint grin. He said with frightening, icy calmness, 'Well, maybe not . . . we might just hang you – most rustlers are hanged when they're caught, aren't they?'

The four Cottonwood men were used to being in a position to intimidate other men, and did not like to admit to, or display fear – but there was something in Lonzo's calm manner that brought a trace of fear to the faces of all four prisoners. Lonzo's real intention was to take the four men back to the ranch for Caleb to deal with, but he hoped that by threatening to hang them, that he might be able to get them to admit that they had been rustling Caleb's cattle, *and* on the orders of their boss, Bart Jarvis.

'You're bluffing!' Burdett scoffed, trying to fight his rising panic, 'You can't prove we've been doing any rustling!'

Lonzo grinned icily, 'We don't have to prove it. We need only hang you.'

His words caused some alarmed muttering between Roebuck, Slater and Gooch, and Archie Burdett's face paled considerably. He felt an emotion similar to terror – an emotion he wasn't used to feeling, though he tried not to show it – and gave a loud snort. Leroy wasn't happy at the thought of hanging the four men, but he sensed that Lonzo was bluffing, and didn't say anything.

Seth Roebuck was the first of the four Cottonwood men to give way to his fear. He knew of Leroy's friendly nature, and began frantically to beg him not to hang them. Leroy felt very disturbed by Roebuck's frantic pleas, but he kept his faith in Lonzo and said nothing. Roebuck's desperate pleading to Leroy exacerbated the fear that his three cohorts were already feeling, and Burdett told him angrily to shut up.

Roebuck went quiet, but only for a moment. He then began to tremble uncontrollably, and cried out, 'You gotta show us some mercy!'

Roebuck's display of fear and trembling gave Lonzo an idea: maybe if he threatened to hang Roebuck before the other three men, he might be able to terrify him enough to confess to the rustling, and to also implicate his boss, Bart Jarvis.

Lonzo said coldly to the quivering Roebuck, 'All I *gotta*

do is hang the four of you, and because I'm sick of listening to your pathetic voice, you'll hang first!'

Roebuck began to wail and stepped away to the side, and Leroy had to grab hold of his arm to stop him from running away. While Leroy kept hold of Roebuck, Lonzo turned his attention to the other three Cottonwood men. In what seemed like one lightning fast movement, Lonzo pushed Burdett, Slater and Gooch one after the other to the ground by shoving them hard in the chest area.

The three men landed on their backs with cries of surprise and pain. Lonzo swooped down next to them, and using some of the strips of rope that Leroy had left lying on the ground, tied their feet tightly together. He then told them it would be their turn to be strung up after he and Leroy had finished hanging Roebuck.

Lonzo straightened up, and caught hold of Roebuck's other arm in a powerful grasp. He looked for a moment into Leroy's eyes, and a kind of understanding passed between them: Lonzo knew that Leroy would go along with his pretence to hang Seth Roebuck.

Roebuck howled and struggled in the grip of the two men. Leroy glanced to the right of him at the cottonwood trees where Slater and Gooch had previously been firing from.

'We can hang Roebuck in those trees,' he said to Lonzo, adding that the horses belonging to three of the Cottonwood men were most likely still tethered there.

Roebuck's frantic cries got louder as he writhed in the hold of Leroy and Lonzo, and he looked down at his three trussed-up companions as though begging them to do something. His three friends squirmed and wriggled in

118

their bonds and tried to heave themselves up into a sitting position, but they couldn't manage it, so lay on their backs and sneered up at Leroy and Lonzo, trying to mask their obvious fear.

Holding Roebuck's arms tightly, Leroy and Lonzo began to drag him over to the trees. Roebuck's wailing became so loud that it almost drowned out the sound of approaching hoofbeats. Lonzo drew out his gun as three riders came into sight, galloping towards them along the rock-strewn trail.

Seth Roebuck went silent, and all four Cottonwood men felt a sudden and frenzied surge of hope that maybe the oncoming riders might intervene in the hanging. The riders galloped closer, and the desperate hope of the Cottonwood men turned to despair as the riders were soon recognized as Caleb Baxter, Marvin Kilbey and another of Caleb's ranch hands, red-haired Cain Jago. Cain was the brother of Trent Jago, the sheriff of the town of Vernal, which was the nearest town to Caleb's ranch.

Lonzo put his gun away, and Caleb, Kilbey and Jago pulled their horses to a stop near to Leroy, Lonzo and their four captives, and dismounted. Caleb was beaming with delight as he looked down at Burdett, Slater and Gooch, who lay on their backs tied up and unable to move, and at Seth Roebuck who was held in the grip of Leroy and Lonzo.

'So you caught them!' he shouted excitedly to Leroy and Lonzo. He was too elated at the capture of the Cottonwood men to notice Leroy's wounds.

'You gott'a help me, Baxter!' a desperate Seth Roebuck suddenly cried out to the ranch owner, 'They're gonn'a

119

hang me!'

'Is that right?' Caleb asked of Leroy and Lonzo, 'Are you going to hang him?'

'We sure are,' Lonzo answered firmly, 'These men were trespassing on your land, and they were probably going to steal some more of your cattle,' and he pointed to the nearby cottonwood trees: 'They got their horses in those trees, and that's where we're taking Roebuck – we was aiming to hang him first and then the others. . . .'

'You can't let them do it, Baxter!' Roebuck begged him, 'You gott'a stop them!'

Burdett, Slater and Gooch again tried in vain to heave themselves up into a sitting position. They no longer tried to hide their fear as they, too, implored Caleb to save them from being hanged.

Caleb smiled again with much enjoyment. It amused him to see the four usually tough and menacing Cottonwood men in such a helpless position, and to hear them begging him to save their lives.

But Caleb knew Leroy and Lonzo well, and he guessed they were bluffing about hanging the four men, and that their plan was to frighten them into confessing to the rustling. So rubbing his hands together he said enthusiastically to Leroy and Lonzo, 'Well then men, let's get on with it!'

Roebuck began to wail hysterically, and cried in desperation to Caleb, 'You can't hang me! You can't hang any of us, we were only doing what Jarvis wanted us to do. He ordered us to rustle your cattle!'

Caleb felt a flutter of excitement when Roebuck mentioned Bart Jarvis. He was very eager to see the end of

Jarvis and his ranch hands, and their countless terrifying activities at Brown Hole.

'Are you saying that you were acting on your boss's orders?' Caleb asked the wailing Roebuck.

'Yes, yes!' Roebuck sobbed. He sagged to his knees as Leroy and Lonzo held on to him.

'And', Caleb asked, 'are you willing to admit that fact to Sheriff Jago in Vernal if I take you there instead of hanging you?'

'Yes!' Roebuck sobbed again.

Caleb looked down at Burdett, Slater and Gooch, 'Are you three also willing to admit that you were acting on Jarvis's orders?'

The three men did not answer him straightaway. They knew that Bart Jarvis would not take kindly to being betrayed, but after Caleb threatened to hang them on the spot, Slater and Gooch, and finally Archie Burdett, grudgingly assured him that they would admit to the sheriff in Vernal that they were acting on Jarvis's orders.

Smiles of satisfaction passed between Leroy, Lonzo and Caleb Baxter. They had got what they wanted, a confession to the rustling, and a confession that implicated Bart Jarvis, the Cottonwood ranch owner. However, Caleb's smile turned to a frown as he noticed Leroy's torn and blood-stained clothes, and his numerous cuts and gashes. 'What happened to you?' he asked his ranch hand.

Leroy started to answer him, but then went quiet as suddenly he felt very weak, and he had to let go of Roebuck's arm.

Lonzo spoke up and said to Caleb, 'Maybe you should ask Burdett about what he did to Leroy.' Lonzo didn't say anything else, but he didn't have to. Caleb realized from what little he had said, that Burdett must have done something really bad to Leroy, and he almost changed his mind about hanging the four Cottonwood men.

Around ten minutes later, the four had been hoisted up into the saddles of their horses. Their hands were still tied, and their feet were tied together under the bellies of their horses. Caleb and his two ranch hands, Kilbey and Jago, were taking the four men to Jago's brother, Sheriff Trent Jago in Vernal.

As the four scared-looking men sat helpless on their horses, Caleb asked Burdett about what he had done to Leroy. Burdett would not tell him, but Roebuck, who was still feeling quite terrified of being hanged, blurted out to Caleb about how Burdett had tried to kill Leroy by dragging him along the ground behind his horse, and how Lonzo had suddenly galloped on to the scene and saved Leroy with his amazing shooting skills.

Caleb was outraged at what Burdett had done to Leroy, and he burst out furiously to the four men, 'If any one of you four fails to admit to Sheriff Jago in Vernal that Bart Jarvis ordered you to rustle my cattle, then me and my ranch hands will break into the jail and lynch you, and I don't think Sheriff Jago will try to stop us!'

Caleb then left Kilbey and Jago to guard the four men. He was still feeling irate as he walked over to speak to Leroy, who was sitting on a boulder at the side of the trail. Lonzo had gone to look for Leroy's horse, which seemed to have strayed. Caleb stared anxiously at Leroy. He looked weak and in pain, and his wounds needed to be cleaned up.

It was quite obvious to the ranch owner that Leroy wasn't fit enough to ride back to the ranch, and that he would probably have to stay at the line shack for several days to rest and recuperate, and he did not want Leroy to stay at the shack alone. Caleb felt sure that Leroy wouldn't object to Lonzo's company for another week or more. The astute rancher had noticed that the two men seemed to have formed a kind of friendship. He was also equally sure that the aloof but capable Lonzo would look after Leroy *and* his cattle.

Caleb waited for Lonzo to come back with Leroy's horse, and then he told the two men to stay at the shack until Leroy felt well enough to ride back to the ranch. He also told Lonzo to get word to him if Leroy started to feel worse, and he would send for a doctor. Lonzo gave him a curt nod.

Caleb started to walk away, but turned back as he remembered something that Roebuck had said to him. He looked thoughtfully at Lonzo for a second, and then said, 'Roebuck told me about your fast and impressive shooting when you galloped up to save Leroy. I never knew you could shoot like that. . . .'

Lonzo cursed to himself. He did not want Caleb or anyone else at Browns Hole to find out that he was the Sundance Kid. The last thing he wanted was a reputation as a gunman. His face was expressionless as he said to Caleb with a shrug, 'I ain't nothing special with a gun, they were just lucky shots. . . .'

'Oh, really!' Caleb said, but looking as though he didn't believe him. Leroy was barely able to stay conscious, but he knew how badly Lonzo wanted to keep secret both his skill with a gun, and the fact that he was known as the Sundance Kid. Although he could only weakly mumble the words, he took Caleb's attention off Lonzo by asking what would happen to the four Cottonwood men when Caleb had handed them over to the sheriff at Vernal.

Caleb said with a sudden grin, 'I'll let Sheriff Jago deal with them, and with Bart Jarvis. They won't be able to go back on their confessions, since the sheriff's own brother heard them confess.'

He cast another thoughtful, almost suspicious look at Lonzo, then turned and strode over to join Kilbey, Jago and his four prisoners.

Lonzo watched his boss walk away; he still felt anxious at what Caleb might be thinking, and then he turned to look at Leroy a little uneasily, wondering how much Leroy had seen of his shooting skills. But Leroy was struggling to stay conscious.

Lonzo sighed, and said, 'Let's get back to the shack before you pass out,' and reached down to help Leroy to his feet.

On the ride back to the shack, Lonzo rode close beside Leroy and had to reach out a few times to hold him steady in the saddle and to lead his horse.

CHAPTER 9

During the next four days, Leroy rested for most of the time. Lonzo did all the cooking, and looked after Leroy very efficiently, as well as riding out regularly on the range to check on the herds of cattle. On the fifth day, Leroy felt recovered enough to ride out for short spells with Lonzo checking over the scattered herds; he was also starting to talk a lot more.

They spent over six more days at the shack before starting the ride back to Caleb's ranch on a very warm afternoon. They did not urge their horses into a gallop, but just trotted along steadily. For the first mile or so while riding along the trail through the grassland, Leroy did not talk much. He was actually doing some thinking. He knew that Lonzo had a restless nature, just like his own, and that he could, at any time – and probably sooner, rather than later – suddenly decide to leave Caleb's ranch without a word to anyone, excepting Caleb.

That thought troubled Leroy, for although he had previously said to Lonzo (and not that long ago) that a partnership between them would be a disaster, he had since changed his mind. He could not deny that he liked Lonzo and felt a unique kindred spirit with him, and he now felt eager to ask him to join into a partnership with himself and Emmett – but first he would have to speak to Emmett.

He felt Lonzo's eyes on him – Lonzo was wondering why he was so unusually quiet.

Leroy turned to look at him and asked, 'How long do you reckon you'll stay working for Caleb?'

Lonzo shrugged, 'I ain't really thought about it.'

Leroy sensed that Lonzo was lying, but he said no more about it.

They had ridden out of the grassland and were trotting their horses through the meadows when Leroy asked Lonzo: 'Do you have any thoughts on what you'll be doing in the future?'

Lonzo grunted, 'I never waste time thinking about the future.'

Leroy laughed. He said cheerily, 'When I think about the future, all I know is that I don't want an ordinary life. Settling down with a wife and kids is not for me . . .' but he stopped speaking as he remembered Amy, the girl he had grown up with and loved.

Lonzo noticed a flicker of sadness in Leroy's eyes, and he remembered seeing it once before, when he said, 'I'm guessing you had a girl at one time . . .'

Leroy smiled, quickly getting over his brief sad moment, 'I did have once, but that was in the past . . . it's like I just said, I don't want a life of settling down with a wife and kids, or of staying in one place and doing the same boring job day after day, I like taking risks and living close to the edge, I want some excitement and danger in my life, even if it means breaking the law at times. . . .'

Lonzo gave a half-smile, and said 'Sounds good to me!'

They rode in silence for a few miles, and were about five miles away from Caleb's ranch when a thought suddenly occurred to Leroy. He looked across at Lonzo with gratitude in his eyes, and said, 'Those so-called *lucky* shots of yours saved my life, and I want. . . .'

'Forget it!' Lonzo sharply cut him off, 'I don't want any thanks!' he lowered his voice and said, 'Besides, I reckon we're even – I owe you for warning me about Gooch and Slater hiding in the trees, and for drawing their fire away from me.'

Leroy smiled, 'Maybe so. . . .' he began – but Lonzo cut him off again, saying 'What did you mean by so-called lucky shots?' he asked curtly, 'They were lucky shots – I ain't no gunman!'

Leroy smiled at him again, 'Don't worry', he said calmly, 'Your secret's safe with me, I already know you're a wizard with a gun, I saw you shoot down those oil lamps at the dance in Jeremiah's eating house.'

Lonzo pulled his horse to a sudden stop, and stared at Leroy with surprise showing in his eyes.

Leroy reined his horse in also, and said quietly, 'I've also guessed that you're the one known as the Sundance Kid . . . .'

The surprise in Lonzo's eyes changed to a brief flare of anxiety. He trusted Leroy, and knew that he would not betray him, but he felt worried that someone else at the dance might also have seen him shoot down the oil lamps, and guessed that he was the Sundance Kid. He asked in a

127

hard voice, 'Did anyone else see me shoot down the lamps?'

'I don't think so,' Leroy said, trying to reassure him, 'I ain't heard any talk of it, and I ain't told a soul that I think you are the Sundance Kid, not even Emmett . . . I did tell Emmett about you shooting down the oil lamps, but he can be trusted not to tell anyone about that.'

Lonzo didn't say anything, just lowered his head and stared down hard at the ground. He didn't look up for several minutes, and Leroy began to worry that Lonzo might be feeling distrustful of him.

Leroy said, 'My knowing that you are the Sundance Kid ain't the reason that I agreed to you coming to the line shack with me – I wasn't trying to take advantage of your shooting skills. . . .'

Lonzo said bluntly without lifting his head, 'Had anyone else said that to me, I wouldn't have believed them.'

Leroy smiled in relief. Lonzo's trust in him meant a lot.

'Anyway,' Lonzo said, looking at Leroy with a slight roguish smile, 'It was really because of my natural charm that you agreed, wasn't it?'

Leroy laughed, 'It surely was!'

They started riding again, and the ranch buildings were in sight when Leroy suddenly burst out cheerily, 'Hey! I'm guessing that Caleb won't want us to do any ranch work until some time tomorrow or even after that, so why don't we just change our horses at the ranch, and then ride out to Jeremiah's eating-house and saloon and enjoy ourselves?'

He didn't know if Emmett would still be working at

Jeremiah's store, but if he was, then he could join them.

Lonzo thought it over for a few minutes, and then he shrugged and nodded. After all that he and Leroy had been through with Burdett and the other Cottonwood men, he didn't like to disappoint him.

Leroy grinned. He hoped that this was the start of the two of them becoming real good friends.

As Leroy and Lonzo rode up to the ranch buildings, they were met by Caleb. The ranch owner had been working in one of the barns when he had spotted them riding up. Caleb, along with Marvin Kilbey and Cain Jago, had only ridden back to the ranch a couple of days earlier after delivering their prisoners to the sheriff in Vernal.

Caleb asked about Leroy's health, then told them to relax for a couple of days before doing any ranch work. Leroy and Lonzo dismounted and let their horses loose in the corral. They took some of their stuff into the bunkhouse, then headed back over to the corral to choose some fresh horses. They were on the point of opening the corral gate when there was a shout behind them: they turned around and saw Emmett hurrying towards them.

Leroy ran up to meet his partner, and laughing and smiling, they hugged each other. As they pulled apart, Leroy rubbed his still slightly painful ribs. Emmett said, 'I was just about to ride out to the line shack to check on you . . . I've only been back at the ranch myself for about thirty minutes, and I've just heard from Marvin about you being injured by Burdett.'

Lonzo stood by the corral gate watching and listening. He saw Emmett take Leroy's arm, and heard him say, 'I know I've only just got back from there, but I reckon you're in need of a good time, so why don't the two of us ride over to Jeremiah's saloon and eating-house – and I'll do all the paying!'

Emmett did genuinely want to spoil Leroy in some way after what his partner had been through, but he was also happy at the thought of seeing Annie again, even though he had not long parted from her.

Leroy smiled his agreement at Emmett, then turned back to Lonzo to ask him to join them. He frowned when he saw that Lonzo had already caught one of the horses in the corral, and that he had led it out through the gate and was putting on the saddle and bridle.

'Lonzo!' Leroy called to him.

Lonzo did not look at him, he just swung up into the saddle of the horse.

Leroy stepped hurriedly towards him before he could ride away. 'Lonzo!' he shouted out, 'You are welcome to join us!'

This time Lonzo did look at him, and said impassively, 'I'm going for a ride.'

A look of dismay appeared on Leroy's face as Lonzo rode past him and away from the ranch. Emmett saw the way that Leroy was staring after Lonzo and asked, 'Is anything wrong?'

Leroy shook his head.

Emmett, though, could see how unhappy Leroy felt, and he sighed. He had known for quite a while that the time would eventually come when Leroy would ask him how he felt about Lonzo joining into their partnership.

Emmett said, 'Why don't you ask him to join into our

partnership if that's what you want?'

Leroy turned to look at him in puzzlement, 'What?' he asked.

Emmett smiled, 'I know you feel a kind of kinship with Lonzo, I've known it for a long time, probably even before you were aware of it, and I know you want to ask him to join into our partnership, so I'm saying, go ahead and ask him!'

Leroy just stared at Emmett in surprise, and for a very rare moment, he was lost for words.

Emmett laughed, 'It ain't often you don't know what to say!'

'Are you sure?' Leroy finally managed to ask.

'He did save my life – and yours!'

'That doesn't answer my question.'

Emmett smiled again, 'Well, Lonzo ain't the friendliest guy I ever met, but he's got a lot of nerve, and I honestly don't *dislike* him.'

Leroy smiled. He felt happier already: he had Emmett's blessing to ask Lonzo to join their partnership, now he just had to find the right time to ask him – and he felt the sooner he did so, the better.

CHAPTER 10

It was just after sunset on the Baxter ranch, and dusk was gathering in the sky. Leroy and Emmett had finished all their jobs for the day, and Emmett was full of excitement – he couldn't stop chattering as he and Leroy left the bunkhouse.

Emmett's elation was because Annie had ridden over to the ranch that day to visit him. She was waiting for him in the ranch house and they were going for a walk. They often went for walks in the twilight when she visited him at the ranch, and she would then stay overnight at the ranch house.

Leroy smiled at Emmett's happiness, but deep down, he was really feeling very dejected. Four days had passed since Leroy and Lonzo had left the shack and returned to the ranch, and Leroy had still not found the right time to ask Lonzo to join into his partnership with Emmett – in fact, even though they shared a bunkhouse, he hadn't spoken much to Lonzo since they had arrived back at the ranch. Lonzo seemed to be purposely avoiding him – whenever he tried to talk to him, he always seemed to find some excuse to walk away, and every time that Leroy visited the library room, Lonzo had not been there. Inwardly, Leroy believed that Lonzo's reason for avoiding him was because he did not want to get too involved with anyone.

Leroy broke into Emmett's excited chattering, saying, 'I think I'll head down to the corral and take out one of the horses.'

Leroy would often go for a ride at night. He liked to ride through the scrubland beyond the ranch buildings. So the partners split up, Emmett hurrying off happily to the ranch house, while Leroy started to stroll down to the corral.

Outside the bunkhouse were a couple of wooden benches, and seated on one of these, Lonzo watched Leroy stroll past him on his way to the corral. Lonzo was dressed in his usual black attire, and wasn't too visible in the growing shadows of dusk.

He *had* been deliberately avoiding Leroy ever since they had got back from the line shack, and he was doing this because he had made up his mind to leave the ranch in a few days' time, and he didn't want the bond that he had formed with Leroy to get any stronger. But as he watched Leroy wandering down to the corral, he could tell by the way he was walking that he was feeling very troubled about something. He sighed, and guessed that it was probably his deliberate avoidance of him that was worrying him, and he decided to stay put on the bench and not walk away, not even if Leroy looked back and saw him.

Leroy suddenly halted in his strolling towards the corral and looked back at the benches outside the bunkhouse.

He had felt someone was there, and through the growing darkness he recognized Lonzo sitting on one of the benches. Leroy stared at Lonzo for a few seconds, then began to walk up towards him. He expected Lonzo to get up off the bench and walk away, but to his surprise, he made no attempt to move.

'Hey,' Leroy said with a grin on his face as he approached Lonzo, 'Have you run out of excuses to walk away from me?'

Lonzo grunted, 'I'm sure I'll think of one in a minute.' But he didn't move off the bench, and Leroy sat down beside him. He hoped that Lonzo would stay seated long enough for him to ask him to join into his partnership with Emmett. He waited for a second, then turned to Lonzo and said, 'I want to ask you something, I've been trying to ask you this ever since we came back from the line shack. . . .'

Lonzo chuckled, and he said without looking at Leroy, 'Is this another favour you want to ask me . . . I mean like the one when you wanted me to play the fiddle for Maria?'

'No,' Leroy said, 'I . . .' he paused, trying to find the right words. Lonzo was a difficult man to deal with.

'I promise I won't bite,' Lonzo said in amusement.

'Well . . .' Leroy began casually, 'I have a hunch that you won't be staying working at the ranch for much longer, and me and Emmett will be leaving the ranch soon, too, so I was thinking that maybe. . . .' he paused again.

Lonzo turned his head to stare at Leroy. He suddenly had a feeling that he knew what Leroy was trying to ask. 'OK, so what is it that you are trying to ask me?' he demanded with irritation.

Leroy decided to come straight out with it, and said, while still keeping his voice casual, 'I'm trying to ask you to join into my partnership with Emmett.'

There was an intense silence after he said this, so much so that he felt uncomfortable and turned away.

Lonzo just stared impassively at Leroy: his feeling had been right, he had sensed that this was what Leroy was going to ask him. The silence was eventually broken by Lonzo saying tersely, 'I thought you said that a partnership between us would be a disaster?'

'I did say that,' Leroy turned to look at him, 'But maybe I was wrong. I'm willing to give it a try if you are, and so is Emmett.'

Lonzo's eyes flashed in annoyance, 'I told you before!' he snapped, 'The last thing I want is a partner, I don't like getting too friendly with anyone!'

Leroy said sadly, 'An attitude like that makes for a lonely future.'

'It's my future!' Lonzo snapped again, 'What do you care?'

Leroy turned away with a heavy sigh, thinking maybe he should forget about a partnership with Lonzo and just walk away – but he wasn't ready to give up yet, it was too important to him.

He turned back to Lonzo with a smile and a compelling gleam in his eyes. He said cheerily, 'Let me put it to you another way. I know you like taking risks, and so do I – so why don't you take a risk now, and give a partnership with me and Emmett a try? You can always walk away if it don't work out.'

Lonzo was still feeling annoyed. He *really* did not want

to enter into a partnership with anyone, not even with Leroy and Emmett, but he did feel a kinship with Leroy that was hard for him to ignore, and so was the compelling gleam in Leroy's eyes. He said slowly, 'Well . . . maybe I'll think about it. . . .'

Leroy's face lit up with a happy smile; he glanced towards the horses down in the corral and said, 'Want'a come for a ride with me, partner?'

'No,' Lonzo answered gruffly, 'And I said I'd only *think* about it.'

Leroy grinned, then got up off the bench and started to walk down towards the corral.

Lonzo stayed seated on the bench. He was already thinking that a partnership was too much of a commitment for him to make. He looked round as he heard voices, and saw Emmett and Annie sauntering past him. They were holding hands and clearly lost in a world of their own. The young couple were going for a walk. Lonzo, and almost everyone else at the ranch, knew that Emmett and Annie's usual route was along a narrow and little used track to the west of the ranch buildings, which led to the base of the low-lying hills.

From the shadows of the ranch house, someone else was watching Emmett and Annie walking hand-in-hand: it was the ranch foreman, Deke Hogan. A dark scowl was on his face. For a long time he had felt a strong attraction to Annie, but she had always spurned his advances in favour of Emmett. He had tried to flirt with her several times during the day while she had been at the ranch waiting for Emmett to finish his jobs. She had been polite, but distant with him. She had eventually joined Caleb's wife, Elizabeth, inside the ranch house to get away from the foreman.

Hogan's lustful craving for Annie, and his fury at her rejection of him, had been building all day, and he now began to follow her and Emmett.

Leroy was still in the corral, talking softly to a chestnut-coloured quarter horse, and he smiled as he saw Emmett and Annie walk past. They were oblivious to everything except each other. Leroy watched them walk out of the ranch yard, and then turn west on to the narrow track that led to the base of the hills.

Leroy turned back to the horse, thinking that he would choose this one to ride, when one of the other horses near to him suddenly neighed uneasily. Leroy looked round to see Hogan following rather furtively behind Emmett and Annie.

Lonzo was still seated on the bench where Leroy had left him. He had also seen Hogan walking cautiously behind the young couple. The ranch foreman was trying to keep in the shadows and Lonzo felt uneasy about what might be on Hogan's mind.

Holding hands and smiling at each other, Emmett and Annie strolled along the narrow path, not realizing that Hogan was stealthily following behind them. The path they were following was narrow and winding, and bordered by boulders, tall, tangled bushes and various trees. They sat down on the trunk of a fallen tree at the side of the path.

Emmett looked into Annie's glowing eyes and pulled her closer to him, and she lifted her face to his: they were both trembling with happiness and desire as he bent his head to kiss her – but then their magical moment was cruelly interrupted. Crazy with jealousy, and from seemingly out of nowhere, Deke Hogan flung himself at Emmett, and dragged him to the ground. In seconds he was straddling Emmett, pounding unmercifully at his face and body.

Annie screamed at Hogan to stop, and tried to pull him off. Emmett tried desperately to fight back, but he was no match for the heavy and muscular Hogan.

Ignoring Annie's screams and futile attempts to pull him off, Hogan's fists continued to pound away at Emmett. Emmet lost consciousness, but Hogan carried on hammering blows down on him – until he was dragged off by Leroy, who had rushed as fast as he could to help.

Hogan furiously turned on Leroy as Annie knelt over the unconscious Emmett with distraught cries. Leroy and Emmett were no strangers to fist fights, and they were usually able to hold their own in a physical contest, but they were only young men compared to Hogan, and as yet did not have the solid muscular strength of the foreman.

Hogan swung a huge, bunched-up fist at Leroy, but Leroy sidestepped to avoid the punch, and managed to land a few good blows of his own – but then Hogan struck him twice in the side of the face with terrific force, and he fell to the ground.

Leroy's head was spinning as he hit the ground on his back, and pain seemed to sweep through his whole body. He had still not fully recovered from being dragged along behind Burdett's horse.

Hogan immediately lunged down to straddle Leroy,

and his huge hands fastened round Leroy's throat, his thumbs pressing down on the young man's windpipe.

Leroy writhed weakly on the ground as he tried to pull Hogan's hands away from his throat. The spinning sensation that he had felt only moments ago had diminished, but he was in agony from Hogan's stranglehold. His strength was failing, his vision was fading and he couldn't breathe, while Hogan pressed down on his windpipe harder and harder.

Annie, who was kneeling beside Emmett and trying to stem the bleeding from his wounds with pieces of material that she had torn from her dress, screamed out to Hogan in horror, 'No, Deke, don't kill him!'

Hogan again ignored her. He had despised and resented Leroy Parker for a long time. He was resentful that all the residents of Browns Hole seemed to like Leroy, and of the way that Leroy always excelled in everything that he did at Caleb's ranch.

Leroy's strength was almost gone and his consciousness was clouding over as he still tried weakly to tear away the throttling hands at his throat – then suddenly, through his pain, weakness and diminishing awareness, he heard the sound of running footsteps and of a voice, which he was vaguely aware was Lonzo's, yelling out something.

Lonzo was racing towards Hogan, yelling at him to get his hands off Leroy.

As soon as Lonzo had seen Leroy leave the corral and hurry after Hogan, he had jumped up off the bench and hastily followed him. He now quickly tackled Hogan from behind: grabbing hold of his shoulders, and with all his strength, he tried to haul the big man off Leroy – but he only managed to pull him back a few inches.

Nevertheless Hogan was surprised and disconcerted, and for a brief second his tight grip on Leroy's throat relaxed.

Leroy tried frantically to gulp in some air. But Hogan almost immediately pulled his shoulders free from Lonzo's grasp, and at the same time drove an elbow backwards with tremendous force into his ribs. Lonzo fell back gasping and clutching his side, while Hogan tightened his grip on Leroy's throat again.

But Lonzo was in desperate fear for Leroy's life, and overcoming his own pain, he scrambled to his feet, drew out his gun, and hit Hogan twice, hard across the skull with the barrel. Hogan gave a low moan, and his hands went limp around Leroy's throat as he lost consciousness. His shoulders slumped and his head dropped down – but he did not fall over.

Lonzo held his blood-stained gun in his hands, and for a moment fell victim to the ruthless streak deep in his nature, one that rarely surfaced: now, for an instant, he felt an overwhelming compulsion to strike Hogan violently across the head with his gun again, and to keep hitting the foreman until his skull was smashed in and he was dead.

He took a deep breath to calm himself and to resist this powerful urge, then he dragged Hogan off Leroy, and thrust him aside. He kicked him over on to his back and made sure that he was unconscious. He then went over to Leroy and knelt beside him, and watched quietly as Leroy lay gasping and rubbing his throat.

Leroy was aware of Lonzo kneeling beside him and tried to smile, for even though his consciousness had been fading and his vision had been blurry, he had seen Lonzo strike Hogan across the head with his gun, and he had also seen how hard it had been for Lonzo to stop himself from smashing in Hogan's skull – but knowing that Lonzo had been able to control his ruthless streak only increased Leroy's regard and admiration for him.

It was several minutes before Leroy stopped rubbing his throat and gasping. He felt groggy and his throat hurt. He looked up at Lonzo and tried to say something, but couldn't get the words out; he coughed a few times, then tried to draw himself up into a sitting position. Lonzo helped him to sit up.

Leroy tried to speak again, but could only manage a husky whisper. He squeezed Lonzo's arm: it was his way of saying thanks. He then glanced anxiously through the darkness at Annie and Emmett – he could hear Annie sobbing as she knelt beside the unconscious Emmett, still trying to stem the bleeding.

Leroy attempted to get to his feet to go over to them, but Lonzo gently pushed him back down, and said, 'You stay there, I'll take a look at Emmett.'

As Lonzo stood up to check on Emmett, he first cast a glance at Deke Hogan, who lay unmoving on the ground about three feet away – but he saw no obvious sign that Hogan was regaining consciousness, and turned his back on the foreman to walk over to Emmett and Annie.

In a flash, Hogan sprang to his feet behind Lonzo and drew his gun.

Leroy saw him, and tried to gasp out a warning to Lonzo while reaching for his own gun – but neither were needed.

Lonzo's reflexes and his instinct for danger were as amazing as his speed with a gun. He had sensed the threat from Hogan, and faster than the eye could see or the mind could conceive, he swung round on the spot and his gun belched flame. The bullet tore through Hogan's chest. The foreman grunted in shock and pain, clutched at his chest, staggered back a few inches and fell to the ground on his back.

Lonzo stood looking down at him, saw the blood gushing from his chest wound, and knew that he was dead. He hadn't wanted to kill him, but his reaction had been immediate and involuntary, and in the semi-darkness his reflex shot had been to the chest. For a moment, as he looked down at Hogan, Lonzo felt revulsion at what he had done; he did have a ruthless streak, but that didn't stop him from feeling some disgust at killing someone.

Leroy stared at Lonzo. He felt relieved that he had not been killed, and he marvelled at the man's uncanny instincts, but he also recognized Lonzo's feeling of revulsion at killing Hogan. He tried to talk to Lonzo – he wanted to tell him that it was not his fault that Hogan was dead – but his words came out as an inaudible croak.

Lonzo heard Leroy trying to talk to him, but he didn't even look at him. He was angry at himself for showing emotion, no matter how fleetingly. He turned his eyes away from Hogan and holstered his smoking gun, then started to walk away.

Annie's quiet sobbing could no longer be heard as she knelt beside Emmett. She was staring at Lonzo through the dim shadows as he walked away, momentarily astounded at his incredible instincts and his speed with a gun.

As Leroy and Annie watched him, Lonzo abruptly stopped walking, and his hand closed over his gun: he had heard voices approaching. Leroy and Annie also heard the sound of shouts and running footsteps getting ever nearer to them, and along with Lonzo, they stared intently into the darkness.

The three of them relaxed as they recognized some of the voices, and a few seconds later Caleb Baxter, Marvin Kilbey, Cain Jago and a few other ranch hands came running out of the increasing blackness towards them. Caleb immediately knelt at the dead body of Deke Hogan, some of the other men rushed over to help Annie and Emmett, while Kilbey and Jago hastened to help Leroy.

Lonzo pushed his way through them and walked away into the night. Leroy, who was being helped to his feet by Kilbey and Jago, watched him go with worried eyes.

Leroy and Emmett were taken into the ranch house. Emmett was still unconscious, and Caleb sent one of his ranch hands to fetch a doctor who resided in the valley.

The doctor took a look at both Emmett and Leroy. He stitched up some of Emmett's wounds, and he told Leroy to rest for a few days, and not to do too much talking as his throat was badly swollen. To Annie's joy, Emmett regained consciousness a little while later.

Leroy, Emmett and Annie were found beds for the night in Caleb's ranch house, and although the doctor had told Leroy not to do too much talking, he insisted on giving a full account in croaky whispers to Caleb about how Hogan had brutally attacked Emmett, and about everything else that had happened afterwards.

Leroy was careful not to mention Lonzo's speed with a gun when telling Caleb about how Lonzo had shot Hogan.

After hearing Leroy's version of events, and then speaking to Annie, Caleb went outside to speak to the ranch hands who were waiting out there for news of the injured; he said 'Well men, I'm pleased to tell you that luckily, Leroy and Emmett are going to be OK . . . and from what Leroy has told me about what happened, I know that Deke was killed in self-defence, so no action will be taken regarding his death.'

The ranch hands mumbled something about not being bothered about Hogan, none of them had liked him. Caleb then went looking around all the ranch buildings for some sign of Lonzo, but he did not find him.

Sometime later that night, when most people inside the ranch house were sleeping, someone knocked on the ranch-house door and had a sombre chat with Caleb.

Leroy woke late the following morning; his throat seemed to hurt much worse than before. Caleb's wife, Elizabeth, brought him some breakfast, but he only managed to eat a couple of mouthfuls. Elizabeth then told him to stay in bed and rest, but he wanted to try and speak to Lonzo, and after first checking on Emmett, he walked over to the bunkhouse to look for him. However, there was no sign of him there, and Leroy was about to leave the building – but then he noticed that Lonzo's bunk had no blankets, there was only the bare mattress, nor were his clothes or any other items hanging from the hook beside the bed.

Leroy felt a sudden chill sweep through his body: he realized at once that Lonzo must have left the ranch during the night, and for a moment, time seemed to stand still.

He stepped over to the bunk and sat down. He felt crestfallen, and he could only guess that Lonzo must have left because he did not want to stay around to answer any questions about his speed with a gun, and because he was not ready to commit to a partnership.

After a few minutes, Leroy looked underneath the bunk and pulled out a storage box that Lonzo had been using. He lifted the lid to look inside the box – he was hoping that Lonzo might have left him a message. But the box was empty except for a book that he assumed was from Caleb's library.

He heard footsteps, and looked up as Caleb entered the bunkhouse and walked over to him. Caleb stood looking at Leroy for a moment; he could see the sadness on the young man's face, and that his usually bright eyes were moist, and he said quietly, 'Elizabeth told me that you had refused to stay in bed and rest, and I guessed you'd come over here looking for Lonzo. . . .'

Leroy did not say anything.

Caleb said, 'Lonzo came to see me last night and said that he was leaving.'

Leroy lowered his eyes.

Caleb said with some sympathy in his voice, 'I know you'd gotten to like him, I liked him too, and I did tell him that what happened with Deke was not his fault, but he still wanted to leave.'

Leroy did not lift his eyes. Caleb squeezed his shoulder

and said, 'If it makes you feel any happier, he did ask if you were going to be OK before he left.'

Leroy gave a sad groan. He lifted the book out of the box and handed it to Caleb, saying in a hoarse, low voice, 'Lonzo left this book behind, I guess it's one of yours.' He hadn't looked too closely at it.

Caleb took it and had a look, and said, 'No, it ain't one of mine, it must belong to Lonzo.'

Leroy suddenly felt a spark of interest at Caleb's words, and his spirits lifted as he snatched the book out of his boss's hands and looked at it more closely. It was small and leather-bound, and entitled *From the Earth to the Moon* by Jules Verne. It was the same book that Lonzo had been reading in the saloon in Green River when Leroy had first seen him, and the book that he had seen Lonzo reading in Caleb's library.

Leroy started to feel a lot more cheerful – his eyes began to glow and a happy smile appeared on his face. Lonzo had left him a message after all.

He knew that Lonzo must have left him the book as a message. A message that told him that, sooner or later, he was destined to meet the plain-speaking and aloof Lonzo again.

CHAPTER 11

It would be over two years, however, before Leroy met Lonzo again.

After leaving Caleb's ranch, Lonzo found work at a ranch in Utah, and while working at the ranch he met up with a couple of outlaws. He was an eager listener to their stories about their bank and train robberies, and the outlaw hideout of Hole in the Wall in Wyoming. Lonzo eventually left the ranch with the two outlaws, and rode with them to the Hole in the Wall.

Leroy and Emmett left Caleb's ranch about three months after Lonzo. They went to work on the ranch of another friend of theirs, a man named Duke Garrison, also someone they had worked for in the past. Garrison's ranch was also located in Browns Hole, to the south of the Green River and at the base of Diamond Mountain.

It was widely known throughout the valley that Duke Garrison was involved with outlaws and in rustling, but unlike Bart Jarvis of the Cottonwood Ranch, Garrison did not rustle livestock from the inhabitants of Browns Hole, and because of this, he was accepted in the valley, and his lawless ways were overlooked. He allowed outlaw gangs to live in cabins on his land as long as they did not commit any crimes in Browns Hole.

Inevitably, while working for Garrison, Leroy and Emmett were soon taking part in the rustling and other unlawful activities that Garrison, and some of the outlaws residing in the cabins, were involved in.

As well as being a ranch owner, Duke Garrison also owned a butcher's shop in the Wyoming town of Rock Springs, and Leroy would sometimes help out in the shop. As a result of this he acquired the nickname of 'Butch'.

Leroy and Emmett worked as ranch hands for Duke Garrison for a couple of months, and then they moved into one of the outlaw cabins that were on his land and became members of an outlaw gang. At first there was no actual leader of this gang, but the other members quickly noticed that Leroy was a smart thinker and that he had a natural flair for leadership – and soon Leroy became the leader of the gang, with Emmett as his second-in-command.

Under Leroy's leadership, the gang successfully robbed a bank and then a train in Denver, Colorado. At this point Leroy began to worry that his lawless ways might bring shame on his family, who were honest, hard-working people, and so he changed his name. Thus Robert Leroy Parker from Utah became known as Butch Cassidy the outlaw. He chose the name Butch after the nickname that he had been given while working in Garrison's butcher's shop, and the name Cassidy in honour of Mike Cassidy who had taught him so much about cattle, guns and horses – and it was a name he had sometimes used before.

Leroy – alias Butch – did not forget Lonzo, and Emmett would often see him in the cabin at night reading the Jules Verne novel by the light of an oil lamp.

Emmett did not forget Annie, either. He met up with her at the eating house in the valley as often as he could, and she would always beg him to leave the outlaw gang, and told him that she would never marry an outlaw. Her words caused Emmett to do some serious thinking, as he did not want to lose her.

Butch and Emmett had been committing lawless acts with their outlaw gang for several weeks, when one night in their cabin as Butch sat reading the Jules Verne novel, he noticed that Emmett seemed to have something on his mind, and as Butch was about to ask what was wrong, Emmett suddenly blurted out that he was giving up his outlaw life and that he was going to marry Annie.

Butch's face turned sad, and Emmett said quietly, 'I'm sorry, but I don't want to lose Annie.'

They both felt very emotional as they knew it meant the end of their partnership and they did not speak for several minutes. Finally, Butch cleared his throat and tried to smile as he said, 'I'm glad you've found happiness with Annie.'

Emmett felt worried about his friend's future, and he tried to talk him into going back to Amy and settling down – but settling down and living an ordinary life was not what Butch wanted.

The outlaw gang led by Butch split up not long after

Emmett had left, and Butch soon formed another part-nership with an outlaw named Matt Warden, who was from the same part of Utah that Butch was from. Butch still kept his outlaw cabin at Browns Hole, but he and Matt bought a ranch on the outskirts of the Wind River valley town of Dubois, Wyoming, and ostensibly they went into the horse-breeding business – but the horse breeding was a cover up for their real activity, which was rustling cattle and horses.

Around five or six months later, however, Matt Warden was to cause the downfall of their rustling operation. Matt was in a saloon in Dubois one afternoon: he was drinking heavily, and he boasted loudly to a saloon girl about the rustling activities that he and Butch were really engaged in. He was overheard by a deputy who happened to be in the saloon at the time, and when Matt left the saloon later that afternoon and started riding back to the ranch, he was followed by the local sheriff and four deputies.

The lawmen could have arrested Matt at any time, but they chose to follow him back to the ranch because they also wanted to capture Matt's accomplice, Butch. Matt, who was still drunk from the alcohol he had consumed, did not realize he was being followed, and the sheriff and his deputies followed him for over eight miles to the ranch.

Matt dismounted outside the ranch house. He was still quite intoxicated, and as he got down from his horse he fell over, and was trying to get to his feet when the sheriff and his deputies rode up and pointed their guns at him. Matt was quickly arrested and handcuffed, and while two deputies stayed with him, the sheriff and his other two deputies cautiously entered the small, two-room ranch house with their guns drawn. They found Butch asleep on a lower bunk bed in the back room.

Butch was roughly awakened and hauled to his feet by the lawmen. He tried to put up a fight, but he was soon overpowered, his hands were handcuffed behind his back and he was taken outside to join Matt.

Butch was sentenced to serve twelve months in the Wyoming Territorial prison in Laramie. Matt Wardon somehow managed to convince everyone at his trial that he had been coerced into the rustling by Butch, and he received only a six months sentence.

On a crisp and cool morning in March, twelve months later, Butch was released from prison after serving his time. He already had a plan in mind, which was to ride back to his cabin at Browns Hole to form another outlaw gang. He purchased a horse and a gun in Laramie, and then started on his ride back to Browns Hole. The ride to the valley would take him about a week, and through the Medicine Bow mountain range. He stopped over in a few towns along the way.

On riding into the valley of Browns Hole, Butch stopped at the general store of Jeremiah Baxter to speak to Emmett.

Annie and Emmett had got married while Butch had been in prison, and his former partner was now working at the store. Emmett tried again to talk Butch into settling down with Amy or some other girl that he might fancy; he added with a smile, 'Maria's been asking about you!'

Butch said, 'I ain't got no intention of settling down,

I've got other plans.'

Emmett asked, 'What other plans?'

Butch grinned, 'I'm gonn'a start getting another outlaw gang together.' He sighed as he remembered his unfortunate partnership with Matt Wardon, 'I hope to find another partner like you . . . I mean a partner I can *really* trust.'

Emmett smiled. It was a rather odd smile, as though he was hiding a secret. 'Well,' he said to Butch, 'Maybe that won't take you as long as you think. . . .'

Butch was feeling tired as he left Emmett and rode to the south of the valley and the outlaw cabins on Duke Garrison's ranch land. It had been a long ride from the prison in Laramie. He rode past some of the other outlaw cabins and corrals that were partially concealed amongst tall trees and clusters of silvery-grey shrubs before riding up to his own cabin.

He let his horse loose in the corral that was attached to the side of the cabin, and then holding his saddle-bags and other gear, he entered the small timber building. The cabin wasn't too dusty or untidy inside, as both Duke Garrison and Emmett had been looking after it while Butch had been living on his ranch near Dubois with Matt Wardon, and serving his time in prison.

The cabin had two rooms. One was small and was used as a bedroom. A curtain divided the two rooms.

Butch took some cans of food and other provisions that he had purchased at the general store from out of his saddle-bags, and he also took out the book that Lonzo had left behind at Caleb Baxter's ranch.

Butch felt a sudden sadness as he looked at the book. He hadn't seen Lonzo for just over two years, but during that time he had heard plenty of stories about the man now known throughout the west, and possibly far beyond, as the Sundance Kid – stories about the Kid's speed with a gun and his tough nature, and also that he was suspected of robbing several banks and trains with an outlaw gang based at the outlaw hideout of Hole in the Wall.

Butch sighed. He could only surmise that Lonzo must have given up trying to keep secret the fact that he was also known as the Sundance Kid.

He got busy storing away the cans of food and other items, and cleaning out the small wood-burning stove. He placed a couple of logs and some kindling inside the fire chamber of the stove, but he felt too tired to light a fire and cook a meal, and instead ate some beef jerky and some dried fruit.

Afterwards, he drew aside the curtain that separated the two rooms of the cabin and went into the small room that was used as a bedroom.

There were two beds in the room, each bed had a mattress and blankets. Butch lay down on one of the beds, and before he fell asleep he thought briefly about the odd smile that Emmett had given him, and wondered what it meant.

The next morning when Butch woke up, the sun's rays were already glinting through the cabin's bedroom window. He squinted in the sunlight and moved off the bed. He felt a strange feeling of loneliness and told himself that prison had done that to him, made him feel vulnerable in some way, and that it was best to keep busy.

His first job, he decided, would be to find a bucket and fetch some water from a nearby creek. He found a tin bucket outside the cabin near to the corral, and was about to walk the few yards past the corral to the creek just beyond when he noticed that there were two horses in the corral instead of just his own.

The other horse was a black stallion. Butch stared at it for a second in puzzlement, then shrugged, and assumed that maybe an outlaw from one of the other cabins had put it in the corral for some reason. Gripping hold of the handle on the bucket, Butch started to walk towards the creek.

It was then that he heard a whistling sound. He stopped walking and listened – and yes, it was definitely a whistling sound, and it seemed to be coming from a dense group of trees on the left side of the cabin.

Butch glanced towards the left of the cabin. He could vaguely see a dark shape amongst the trees – and then, as he listened to the whistling, he realized who the black horse in the corral belonged to, and his face suddenly lit up with the brightest of smiles and he inwardly started to cheer.

The tunes being whistled were 'Oh Susanna' and 'Sweet Betsy from Pike', with a few odd notes in places. Butch dropped the bucket and cried out ecstatically, '*Lonzo!*'

The dark shape began to move towards him along the side of the cabin, and the shape materialized into Lonzo, alias the Sundance Kid. He was dressed all in black as usual, but there was a sandy moustache on his upper lip. He had a half-smile on his face as he walked up to Butch and said impassively, 'I see you still remember our signal!'

Butch beamed at him – he was so glad to see him that he quickly charged forwards to give him a huge hug. Sundance didn't pull away from the hug, but he didn't hug Butch back, just gave his arm a quick squeeze.

Butch stepped away, still beaming with happiness.

Sundance said, 'Most people ain't usually *that* pleased to see me!'

Butch stood smiling at him for a moment, and he felt again the kindred spirit between them. He knew that Sundance must have purposely sought him out for a reason – he was probably aware that he was now known as the outlaw Butch Cassidy, and he hoped that Sundance was now ready for a partnership.

Sundance said with a slight smile, 'I've been hearing a lot of things about you. . . .'

Butch grinned, 'So I take it you know I'm known as Butch Cassidy now!'

Sundance said with his smile still faintly visible, 'Well . . . from all that I've heard about Butch Cassidy, the bank and train robbery, it wasn't hard for me to work out that Butch Cassidy was really Leroy Parker, the young man who didn't want an ordinary life. . . .'

Butch laughed, 'I've been hearing a lot of things about you, too! I've heard you've been riding with outlaw gangs from Hole in the Wall . . .' he looked at Sundance a bit studiously, 'I'm guessing that you gave up trying to keep your identity as the Sundance Kid a secret, and that most of the folk here in Browns Hole know you as Sundance now.'

Sundance's eyes grew serious, and he said, 'I wasn't able to stop it from becoming widespread knowledge that I was also known as the Sundance Kid. While I was at Hole in the Wall, I met up with a man who had known me in prison, and this man soon spread it around the hideout about my other identity – and from Hole in the Wall, it leaked out to other places.'

Butch stared at him a little sadly, and said, 'I know it ain't what you wanted, but something like that was bound to happen sooner or later – and your reputation with a gun is just gonn'a keep on growing, you know that, don't you?'

Sundance shrugged, and said 'I know, and it's just something I'm gonn'a have to live with, now that I've chosen the outlaw life. . . .'

They both went quiet for a moment as they thought about the consequences of being outlaws.

Butch then looked over at the cabin; he was starting to feel hungry and he wanted some breakfast.

'Hey', he said cheerily to Sundance, 'I don't know if you're aiming to stay here for a while, but I'm hungry!' He picked up the bucket, and looked over at the cabin again, 'And I'm hoping that you're still a good cook, so why don't you go and cook us some breakfast while I fetch some water from the creek?'

Sundance stared down at the ground for a second, and then he lifted his head to look at Butch, and said in his usual blunt way: 'It kind'a depends on you if I stay here for a while. I'm here because I want to know if you're still interested in the partnership you asked me about over two years ago.'

Butch felt himself cheer inwardly again. He *definitely* was still interested in a partnership with Sundance, and he knew that Sundance was serious – but he decided to be a bit cautious, and he said, 'Are you sure a partnership is what you want? You walked out on our last partnership before it had even begun, *and* without a word to me!'

'That ain't exactly how it was!' Sundance snapped. He looked annoyed, 'I only said that maybe I'd *think* about joining into a partnership with you and Emmett, and we never shook hands on it or anything, and I did leave you a message!'

'Oh, yes!' Butch remembered with a laugh, 'The book!'

Sundance said sharply, 'Are you still interested in a partnership with me, or am I wasting my time?'

Butch smiled at him a little fondly, and said, 'You are not wasting your time, I surely *am* still interested in a partnership with you, we are kindred spirits you and I. . . .'

Sundance's annoyance started to disappear as he smiled at Butch's reference to them being kindred spirits.

Butch then asked him, 'What made you seek me out now to ask about a partnership? I mean, it's been over two years, like you said?'

Sundance gave a slight shrug and said curtly, 'Let's just say I've realized that if I'm going to be an outlaw, then I do need a partner to work with, and it has to be someone I can trust – and I already know that I can trust you.'

Butch grinned, and said, 'The partnership will be just between me and you now, as Emmett got married to Annie and has settled down.'

Sundance said, 'I know, I've seen Emmett at the store, I've been working for Duke Garrison while I was waiting for you to get out of prison.'

Oh! Butch thought to himself, so that was why Emmett

had given him that odd smile!

Sundance looked in the direction of the cabin, and said briskly, 'Well, now that we've sorted out our partnership, I'd better go and cook us some breakfast,' and he started to walk towards the cabin.

Butch caught his arm and held out his hand, and said, 'I think this time we should shake hands on our partnership!'

Sundance smiled as he took Butch's offered hand, and said, 'I hope you know what you're taking on. I ain't an easy person to get along with. . . .'

Butch said, 'I *do* know what I am taking on: I'm taking on a partner I trust with my life – and anyway, I ain't no angel, I got my bad points too!'

Sundance nodded, 'Yeah, you talk too much!'

Butch laughed, and said with happy enthusiasm, 'Well, partner, are you ready for a life less ordinary for however long it may last, and wherever it may take us?'

'You bet!' was Sundance's answer.

CHAPTER 12

The night had seemed endless, and as the first light of dawn filtered through the window of the bedroom, Butch still felt half crazy with worry as he sat beside the bed where his wounded partner lay in the cabin home of their friend, Jerome Arnott. He had tried to take his mind off his worry by narrating half out loud to himself for most of the night, the story of how he had first met Sundance, and how their partnership had begun.

The hours passed by with no sign of Sundance waking up. Fear and dread still tore at Butch's heart, and he kept telling his partner that he had to pull through. Several times he found himself weeping in despair.

It was around mid-morning when Jerome Arnott entered the room; he had just got back from Buffalo. He had ridden into the town to try and find out if Luther Greeley, the man who had shot Sundance, was still there.

'You can stop worrying about Greeley coming after you,' Arnott said to Butch, 'I've just spoken to some of the townspeople in Buffalo, and they told me that Luther Greeley has been shot dead by the sheriff.'

Butch knew that he should feel some sense of relief

from Arnott's words about Greeley, but at that precise moment, he did not.

Arnott then took a look at Sundance. He noticed that there had been no fresh bleeding through the bandages, and Sundance's breathing seemed a lot easier. He smiled at the worried and tired-looking Butch: 'And you can stop worrying so much about Sundance, he's breathing easier and he should wake up soon.'

Arnott left the room, and around an hour later, as Butch stared down at his partner through sore, red-rimmed eyes, the wounded Sundance suddenly stirred and opened his eyes. He gasped a few times in pain, and looked up weakly at Butch before giving him a faint impression of a smile of recognition. Butch squeezed his partner's arm in relief. He told Sundance they were in Jerome Arnott's cabin, and that he had taken him there after Luther Greeley had shot him.

'Do you remember Greeley shooting you?' Butch asked his partner. Sundance muttered a weak reply.

'Well, we don't have to worry about Greeley any more,' Butch told him, 'The sheriff in Buffalo shot him dead.'

Sundance muttered something that sounded like good.

'You gave me quite a scare, partner,' Butch said, 'I thought you were never going to wake up!'

Sundance murmured weakly, 'I had to wake up, if only to stop you from telling any more stories. . . .'

'You heard me?' Butch felt surprised and a little embarrassed.

'I heard some of it,' Sundance murmured as he looked at Butch, 'and like I always said – you talk too much!'